OCEAN'S HAMMER

A QUINTERO AND HOYT ADVENTURE

D. J. GOODMAN

SEVERED PRESS
HOBART TASMANIA

OCEAN'S HAMMER

WWW.SEVEREDPRESS.COM

ISBN: 978-1-925342-63-5

1

True to the weather reports, the sky was nearly cloudless. The temperature was in the high eighties, right in that sweet spot between too cold for their required attire and hot enough to bake their group on the deck of their boat. There was a stiff wind blowing in the odor of brine off the ocean but otherwise the weather was great. *What a perfect day for a little piracy*, Maria Quintero thought.

She chided herself for thinking of it in such melodramatic terms. Everything they were planning to do today was legal, at least in the most technical terms. At the very least there wouldn't be any court that would prosecute them. But *piracy* was the more exciting term and she embraced it, at least for now.

Down by the beach, Maria could see the rest of the One Planet volunteers gathering at the dock where they waited for her and Kevin to join them. According to their intel, they only had a limited opportunity to reach their target so they were supposed to be on a tight schedule. It looked like everyone was conforming to that schedule except Kevin himself.

Maria waved at the others to signal they would be down shortly, then came in off the deck to Kevin's living room. Kevin Hoyt's home was modest compared to some of the other homes in this particular stretch of the Baja Peninsula but that didn't mean it was cheap. Few other marine biologists would be able to afford a home like this, but then few other marine biologists had turned their adventures into world-wide bestselling memoirs.

"Kevin, honey?" she called as she approached his office. "It looks like everyone else is here. We need to get moving with the supplies if we're going to be on time."

The door of his office was partially closed, which in itself was odd. He was a very open person by nature and in the year that the two of them had been dating, she'd never seen him close any doors against her, not even when he was going to the bathroom. "Kevin?" she asked as she gently knocked on the door.

"Are you sure?" Kevin asked. Maria was pretty sure that wasn't intended for her, so she quietly pushed the door open. He was at his desk with a phone cradled between his ear and his shoulder. All three of his computer monitors were on and he was typing furiously, but from this angle Maria couldn't see the screens. "How many species reported so far?" He turned to the door enough to see Maria and gestured for her to come in but she was obviously the furthest thing from his mind at the moment.

Maria plopped in an overstuffed chair in the corner of his office and stared at him in confusion. Dr. Kevin Hoyt was in his early fifties, over twice Maria's age, so the two of them made an extremely strange couple. Maria came from a comfortably middle-class family in San Francisco where she hadn't wanted for much but had still felt like she owed the world for how lucky she'd been. Kevin, on the other hand, had come from a poor family in the Midwest. He'd never even seen the ocean until he was twenty-nine, which made his meteoric rise to being known as the next Jacques Cousteau all the more startling. Physically, he was an impressive specimen with a body obviously shaped by getting his hands dirty on his many ocean expeditions. His red goatee probably looked scraggly and unkempt to anyone else, although Maria knew he spent lots of time in front of the mirror cultivating that look. His beard was a point of pride with him. Privately, he had admitted to her that was because he hadn't been able to physically grow one before he was thirty five, back when he'd still be known as Julie, and he'd started to transition from female to male. While Maria had been unsure how comfortable she was at first with having a relationship with a much older transgender man, she had quickly realized that how she felt about him had nothing to do with what he might or might not have between his legs. The age difference was still strange, though.

"Look, I really can't," Kevin said into the phone with a genuine note of regret. "I'm supposed to be heading out shortly anyway and..." He paused. "I get that. Of course I get that. Everything you're saying makes this seem comparable to the mass beaching in the Bahamas in 2000. But remember that producer guy I was telling you about?"

Maria made sure to pay close attention to his face as he mentioned the producer. This had been a source of tension for them both for the last week. As much as Kevin's fame had come to pay for his research and give him free reign over his own projects, he still occasionally had to ask for grants and loans to keep the *Cameron* afloat. If the producer and his cameraman liked what they saw today and thought it was compelling enough television to turn into a reality show, then he wouldn't even have to worry about those extra expenses anymore. Or at least that was what Maria kept telling him. She was a lot more comfortable with the idea of a camera following them around than he was.

"Yep, today," Kevin said. "No, I don't think so... an illegal shark fishing ship from Japan... yeah, that's him. Up to his old shit yet again."

There was a much longer pause as whoever was on the other end of the phone spoke excitedly and loudly enough that Maria could almost, yet not quite, make out what he was saying. And it was definitely a he, so that narrowed down the possibilities a little bit. When Maria had first decided to take a break from school to come down here and join Kevin's grand adventures on a more permanent basis, she'd had trouble keeping track of all his colleagues and contacts. Now she pretty much knew them all, even counted one or two as her friends. Most of the others she found a tad insufferable. She'd felt the same way about Kevin at first until she had gotten to know him. Still, it was difficult for her socially here when most of the other people she had contact with were not even close to the same age. It was even worse sometimes considering how many of his friends she suspected thought she was sharing Kevin's bed just to get a touch of his fame.

"Well look, this shouldn't take more than a day. Ito knows he's not supposed to be there. It won't take much to get him out of the MPA. Tomorrow I can have some of the OP volunteers going up and down the shorelines with a couple of Zodiacs and I'll personally supervise the removal of any heads we find."

Maria smiled. There would have been a time not too long ago where that phrase would have startled her and made her question what kind of psychopath she was in a relationship with. Now she understood that he was referring to the heads of beached whales and dolphins. If there was a large number beaching themselves then one of Kevin's fellow marine biologists would need them for autopsies.

"Yeah, sure, I'll keep an eye out but we're not going to be that close to the shore for most of the day... All right. I'll have the radio on the *Cameron* if you truly find something you think I need to know... Yeah. You too."

He ended the call before finally acknowledging Maria. "Sorry about that."

"Don't be sorry. Sounded important. Mass beaching?"

"Uh-huh. One or two on the other side of the Sea of Cortez, but mostly here on the Baja side. Multi-species. So far Laguna's confirmed a couple species of dolphins and at least three of whales. Most are pygmy beaked whales, one of which apparently came up on shore right in front of a bunch of tourists in La Paz. None of them knew enough to try to get it back into the water so they just took pictures of it as it died."

Maria was finally at the point in their relationship where she thought she could detect dueling emotions in his voice. On the one hand, he would be upset about the casual disregard for the whale's life. On the other hand, there was the scientist side of him. That was the one that would be excited about so much documentation of such a fresh specimen, especially since the local pygmy beaked whales were such an under-studied population.

"There was even a minke whale, but thankfully that one wasn't anywhere near a population center."

Maria racked her brain. She was getting there when it came to her own studies in marine biology, but she still had a long way to go before she had Kevin's encyclopedic knowledge. Minke whales weren't as common in this area as some of the other species she'd been studying with him. "Why thankfully?"

"Too big. Trying to move it would be too hard without a full team, and it's going to stink to high heaven after it sits for too long."

"Correct me if I'm wrong, but isn't this not the right time of year for some of those species to even be here?"

"It is unusual, yeah." He frowned and stared at what he had been typing on his screen. "Very unusual. Some of them should have migrated north by now. There's no logical reason for them to have stayed." He turned around and looked at a map of the Baja Peninsula and its surrounding waters that he kept tacked to a cork board on his wall. As he stood up from his chair, he took a few pins from a jar near his computer and poked them in, presumably marking the locations of the known beachings. With the exception of the one in La Paz, all of them were north of their current location.

"Is there any idea what caused this yet? Like..." She paused and thought back to some of the reading she had been doing right here in the office. "Like what you were saying about what happened in 2000 in the Bahamas? That Navy sonar thing?"

Kevin stared thoughtfully at the map. US Navy sound experiments in the ocean, used to search for enemy submarines, had been responsible for one of the worst marine mammal beachings in known history. The acoustics played havoc with whales' natural navigation systems, damaging their ability to sense depth and leaving them unable to tell they were going straight for land. After a moment, though, Kevin shook his head.

"That was one of the first things I asked. But that wouldn't make sense. The US Navy doesn't have jurisdiction in these waters, so unless someone else is trying out the same thing then that can't be it." However, he didn't look terribly convinced by his own argument. Turning back to the map, he ran his fingers over a rough black circle he had drawn in the Sea of Cortez not far from their current location.

"I know what you're thinking," Maria said.

"Do you?" He turned back to her and raised an eyebrow.

"You're thinking that whatever caused the beaching is somehow related to whatever the hell's going on at El Bajo."

He nodded but said, "I don't see how it could be. The two events don't seem to have any relation. Just because two unexplained marine events happen in the same region shouldn't mean anything." Yet as he placed more pins in the board Maria couldn't help but notice that, in that whole long sliver of sea, none of the pins were south of that circle.

As fascinating as Maria honestly thought this was, she had to remind herself that they were on a time table. "You can keep working on that later," she said as she stood up. "If you've still got the energy for it then."

He put down the rest of his pins and went over to her for a flirty embrace. "Well I certainly intend to enough energy for more than just that."

She gave him a quick peck on the lips before backing away. "Down boy. I don't care how virile you still are. This is going to be exhausting. It's not every day we get to be pirates."

He frowned in such a way that still somehow managed to be cheerful. "I wish you would stop calling it that. It gives people the wrong idea."

"It's not that wrong of an idea. They're similar."

He made a comical show out of his long-suffering sigh. "Just whatever you do, don't say that in front of the big-shot TV producer."

2

"Yeah, we're basically gonna be pirates," one of the volunteers said directly into the camera. Maria hung back at the beginning of the dock, desperately trying not to laugh as Kevin briskly walked down the dock to stop him before he said anything else. The volunteer in question, a very new addition to the One Planet organization named Kirk Murphy, stood in front of the camera in what was very obviously a rehearsed pose. He was the kind of spiky blond-haired, chiseled physique college boy that just naturally assumed everyone wanted to see his smiling mug all over the TV screen. It hadn't escaped Maria that he just so happened to volunteer for the One Planet Sea Brigade right around the same time the internet had started buzzing about a reality show following the famous Kevin Hoyt and his intrepid crew on the *Cameron*.

"Doug, hi. Glad you could make it," Kevin said, holding his hand out to the short man standing next to the cameraman. Despite his attempts to block Murphy from view, the kid still managed to stay in the middle of the shot.

"Dr. Hoyt, I'm so happy we could finally meet in person," Doug Vandergraf said. While hardly a household name, Maria had been familiar with his work well before he had contacted Kevin about today. He'd produced a number of reality shows on the higher cable channels that, while trashy, Maria still had to admit were somewhat entertaining when there was nothing else to watch. Today was merely intended to be a test of sorts. Maria's understanding was that any interviews or footage Vandergraf got today would be used to create some kind of pitch reel, although she forgot which channel exactly was interested. She wanted to be excited about this, but Kevin was still very much on the fence about the idea. As the star he would have the final say, but at least he was willing to explore the idea.

While this was going on, four other volunteers busied themselves prepping the *Cameron* for departure. The *Cameron* was a heavily modified trimaran superyacht that had begun its life intended for millionaires with way too much time on their hands. Now the deck near the back, previously outfitted with a bar, was instead covered in a complex system of pulleys and winches for a robotic submersible. Below decks the various amenities had been replaced with labs and specimen preservation tanks and freezers. The overall result was cramped but state of the art, the sort of thing Kevin had never been able to afford early in his career. Although she'd felt claustrophobic on it at first, Maria now considered it her home even more so than Kevin's house. If she hadn't been fully dedicated to marine biology before she'd joined him then the *Cameron* had cemented her passion with many nights of beautiful sunsets out on the seas.

Maria knew most of the volunteers well enough. She herself had started out as one, after all. One Planet as an organization was small but respected and Maria had wanted it on her resume. She'd come to spend a couple months studying the impact of overfishing in the Sea of Cortez and stayed when her relationship with Kevin had gone from cordial to flirty to something a lot more intimate. She was on the payroll now officially as volunteer coordinator, even if her actual duties were varied and eclectic. Paulo Gutierrez, the pilot, was the only other paid person on the *Cameron*. Two of the volunteers, Simon and Cindy Gutsdorf, did most of the other boat-related tasks while Monica Boleau assisted in a more science related capacity. The remaining volunteer, Diane Mercer, was helping load equipment and supplies despite her small frame struggling with the weight. Of all the volunteers, she was the one Maria knew the least about. She had joined on with Murphy and, while apparently excited about various ecological issues, didn't appear to know much about what she was doing when it came to boats or biology. Honestly, Maria suspected Murphy had only brought her down with him as a bed warmer. Yet another reason why she was hardly Murphy's biggest fan, but he supposedly came from a wealthy family and, even with all of Kevin's fame, there were still those times when their research needed extra funding. They couldn't afford to turn him away.

While this was going on, Vandergraf and his cameraman conferred with each other. Maria walked up to Kevin and took his hand.

"You look nervous," she said as she picked off a piece of lint from his plain gray t-shirt. She'd met a number of other marine biologists with a penchant for aloha shirts yet Kevin would never wear anything that colorful, even knowing full well what would be going on today.

"I hate being on camera," he said. "Remind me again why we're doing this."

"Just keep reminding yourself that this is all about raising awareness."

"Seems to me I've raised plenty of awareness from behind a word processor."

"Don't be such a grumpy old man. You've got the name recognition, but if the network picks this up you'll reach a whole new audience."

He made a mock expression of indignation. "Why Maria Quintero, I am positively offended. You certainly weren't saying I was old yesterday when we…"

"Oh please for the love of God don't finish that statement."

"Why? Suddenly deciding to become a prude with a camera so close by?"

"No, it's clichéd. Come up with something more original in the future if you ever want me in your bed again."

"Har har," he said. Maria saw that the conversation had loosened him up and smiled. She gave him a playful pat on the butt before going to look at the supplies one last time and make sure they had everything. As she did, Vandergraf and the cameraman approached Kevin.

"Why don't we just do a brief introductory clip to explain what we're doing today?" Vandergraf said.

"Sure. Where do you want to start?"

"Well, you don't really need to introduce yourself, I think. Maybe you should start with why you're here? Why the Baja Peninsula and the Sea of Cortez, out of all the places in the world where you could make your home base?"

"Why not? It's beautiful. And even more important to me, it's rich with biodiversity in a relatively small area. Whales especially…" Maria heard him pause. She looked up from her clipboard, wondering if he would mention the mysterious beaching. Instead, he continued on script. "Many species come down here during mating season. You can stand on the shore and without even going under the water see the unimaginable bounty of... uh, sorry. I'm probably getting a little carried away."

"Carry away all you want. It makes good television."

"Um, right. It's not just the whales, either. It's things like what we're going to hopefully see today, provided our rival doesn't reach it first."

"Sounds like a segue if I ever heard one. Explain to me exactly where we're going."

Maria didn't need to hear any more. Kevin was handling himself fine, if a little dorky, and he didn't need her hovering around. Instead, as he explained today's trip to El Bajo, Maria pulled Murphy away from where he had still been trying to appear in the background and ordered him to go help Gutierrez with any final preparations before launch. Then she went below to do a final inventory of the labs.

Not that she wouldn't have liked to listen to Kevin talk more about El Bajo. The place had suddenly become a marine mystery that piqued the curiosity of every marine biologist in the world. They were simply the ones who were living practically on top of it, and that made it their mystery to attempt to solve. She didn't exactly expect them to have all the answers before anyone else showed up, but she was excited to know they would probably have some.

From the surface, El Bajo looked like nothing other than more sea, completely indistinguishable from anywhere else on the Sea of Cortez. Below the surface, however, El Bajo was a large undersea mount. It was somewhat impressive, if not too much different than other underwater geological formations. What had made El Bajo special in the past wasn't what it was but what called those waters home. Back in the seventies and eighties, before Maria had even been born, El Bajo had been one of the largest known breeding grounds of hammerhead sharks. Scientists had come from all over the world to study them during breeding season, and Kevin told Maria it was a spectacular sight, hundreds of hammerheads circling the mount in an intricate mating pattern that suggested a far more complex social structure than marine biologists had thought possible.

By the time Maria had first joined Kevin down here those days were long gone. Commercial fishing had destroyed the shark population, not just in the Sea of Cortez but throughout the world. Maria had dived down to El Bajo on several occasions last year when she and Kevin had been assisting one of Kevin's colleagues with an experiment to test the long-believed yet never conclusively proved theory that many species of sharks, including hammerheads, navigated by sensing the magnetic fields of the Earth itself. She hadn't seen any hammerheads at all and only a few species of sharks too small to have caught the interest of fishing boats. With every year that passed, it was beginning to look like hammerhead sharks were locally extinct.

Until one week ago.

Maria had nearly finished with the inventory when Gutierrez ran up to her and explained what he had just heard over the short wave radio. A couple of tour boat guides Kevin had paid to keep an eye out for marine traffic a couple miles off the tip of the peninsula had reported in. The ship they had suspected was coming had been sighted ten minutes ago. According to all the chatter Maria and Kevin had been monitoring for the last couple days, the *Tetsuo Maru* shouldn't have reached that point for another hour or so. The Japanese ship was early, which meant the *Cameron* was late.

She rushed back up to the deck to find Kevin and Vandergraf still going through the finer points of shark tracking for the interview. As important as she knew these details might be for the reality show pitch, they were still something that absolutely could wait.

"Kevin, we've got to move now," Maria said. "The *Tetsuo Maru* already passed our checkpoint."

The cameraman apparently sensed the urgency in her voice and immediately started to pack up to get on the trimaran. Kevin also went into a flurry of motion, making sure there wasn't anything they had forgotten, but Vandergraf just looked on at all this with a puzzled expression.

"*Tetsuo Maru*?" he asked. "Is that…"

"You wanted good television," Kevin said. "That'll require an adversary. And you're about to meet them."

3

Maria rejoined Kevin, Vandergraf, and the cameraman on deck once the Cameron was launched and speeding its way to El Bajo. The cameraman had taken out his camera again and was ready to roll once more. Kevin invited her to sit beside him as Vandergraf resumed his questions.

"Okay, so tell me about the villains of this story that we're about to encounter."

Maria interjected before Kevin could open his mouth. "They're not villains. Saying it like that makes it sound like they're mustache-twirling masterminds out to enact some plan to cause global extinction or some shit like that."

Kevin somehow managed to keep smiling, although Maria knew full well how much her opinions on this subject exasperated him. "Now's really not the time for this."

Vandergraf, however, had scented blood in the water and veered right for it. "But Dr. Hoyt just said they're your adversaries, did he not?"

"Which is not the same as villains."

Kevin sighed. "Maria and I agree on a great many things. This is one of the few in which we don't."

"Please explain," Vandergraf said.

Kevin gave Maria a glance as if daring her to answer, but she shrugged and motioned for him to do it.

"It's all because of soup," Kevin said.

"Soup?" Vandergraf asked. The way he said it made it sound like that was the single most improbable thing they could have said. The average person on the street didn't understand just how many mainstream things revolved around the politics of the oceans.

"Specifically shark's fin soup," Kevin said.

"Which I'm assuming is, uh, exactly what it says on the tin?"

"Yep," Maria said. "As Americans we might not understand the big idea, but to the Japanese this is serious business."

"It's not just a delicacy, you see," Kevin said. "It's a wedding tradition. A big one."

"Wait, so these shark hunters only want the fin?"

"Mostly," Kevin said. "They cut off the fin and then dump the shark back into the water. Sort of like poachers in Africa who kill elephants for their ivory or rhinos for their horns. Without their dorsal fin and bleeding profusely, the shark almost always dies."

"That sounds pretty cut and dry terrible to me," Vandergraf said. "How can that be something you two disagree on?" He looked at Maria. "You actually think hunting a species to endangerment just for a tiny part of their body is okay?"

"Hey now, don't go putting words in my mouth," Maria said. "I just don't think it's as straight up black and white as Kevin does. There are many more shades of gray involved."

She tried to ignore him as he rolled his eyes.

"Explain," Vandergraf said. He leaned forward on his knees and had a gleam in his eye like he thought this would make for some great drama with the right editing. Maria suddenly began to wonder if she'd made the right call convincing Kevin to do this.

Maria sighed, then looked as his left hand. "You're married, Mr. Vandergraf?"

He looked down at the gold band on his finger. "Three years."

"Was it a big wedding?"

"Well, I suppose it wasn't small. What does that have to do with—"

"Was that size your idea or your wife's?"

"It was mutual, I guess."

"And was it pretty traditional?"

He sat up straight again, looking like he was maybe beginning to get the point. "There were lots of traditional parts, yes."

"Now imagine something for a second. Imagine, oh, some tiny country in Europe imposing international sanctions on white wedding dresses. How do you and your wife think you would have reacted to that?"

Vandergraf laughed. "We would have told them to go to hell and done it anyway. But there's a problem with your analogy. A white wedding dress doesn't hurt anybody."

"Did you give your wife an engagement ring?"

"Yes..."

"Did it have a big old diamond in it?"

"I sure as hell didn't give my wife a blood diamond, if that's what you're saying. It was entirely ethical."

"Are you absolutely one hundred percent positive on that?"

"I... yes." But he didn't sound sure at all.

"Did you ever really consider that the diamond in your wife's ring might have come at the price of dead people?"

"Maria, for God's sake!" Kevin said.

"I'm sorry. I didn't mean it to come out like I was accusing you of anything," Maria said. "I'm sure there was nothing untoward about where the diamond came from. But you probably didn't think about it, did you?"

"No, not really."

"How many diamonds are sold across the U.S. in a year? I don't know the number, but I'm sure it's huge. That's because culturally, to us, it means love. When a couple decides to get married, only a small number go for something other than a diamond. It's important to us. It's tradition. Now imagine that small country again. They don't know what that diamond means to us, and they don't care. They just know that some diamonds are in fact blood diamonds, and that's enough that they want to put a stop to the whole trade." She paused and thought for a second. "Were you born in the U.S., Mr. Vandergraf?"

"Yes."

"And your parents? Your grandparents?"

"Yes to both."

"And so the only culture you were probably ever exposed to was your own. At least in your formative years, right?"

"Well, I don't know about that..."

"My mother was born in Mexico. My father was born in California, but his parents also immigrated. So we weren't, well, I guess you would say 'integrated' like people whose families have lived there for a couple generations. We had our ways and our customs that weren't generally looked on with a kind eye in our middle class neighborhood where we were the only brown people. We spoke Spanish in private, and occasionally in public. And there would be a person every so often, usually a man, who would see us as we minded our own business, come up to us, and demand that we speak English because 'this was America, fer Chris' sake.' As if us having our own culture was somehow an insult to his own."

Maria leaned back on her seat. "Where we're going today, the area around El Bajo, has recently been designated by the Mexican government as a Marine Protected Area. A preserve, no fishing allowed in an effort to help rebuild the population of a protected shark species which, quite frankly, isn't a danger to anyone who leaves them alone but is locally endangered. So for that reason, I have no problem whatsoever stopping a Japanese fishing vessel that seems determined to break the law. But as far as calling them evil, judging their culture, I think I owe it to them to at least take a step back and consider things might be a little simpler than just right and wrong."

Vandergraf continued to stare at her, completely rapt, for several more seconds before he realized she was finished. "Wow, okay." He turned to the cameraman and whispered something. The cameraman nodded back and Vandergraf looked very pleased indeed. Maria tried not to outwardly sigh. She was pretty sure that entire rant would be part of his pitch to the network.

"Okay then. So this fishing vessel we're going to be chasing, that's the *Tetsuo Maru*?"

"Yes," Kevin said, sounding distinctly relieved that the conversation was going back in a direction he found safe. "Captained by a man named Koji Ito. He's an old veteran at this, one we've run into many times and is more than a little resentful that Americans are telling him where he can fish and what he's allowed to take. Hammerheads are protected anyway and he shouldn't be after them, but even more so at El Bajo, considering the new MPA. According to a source we have on another fishing ship, Ito has been planning to do this just to spite everyone ever since he heard about... well, what's going on."

Vandergraf pulled a smart phone out of his shirt pocket. It wouldn't get a signal this far out on the open water, but he seemed to have notes on it. "What's going on would refer to the incident last week, you mean?"

"That, and everything that has been observed since."

"Could you please explain it all for the camera?"

Kevin hesitated. He'd been debating with Maria whether or not to talk about this where it might get out. Maria had reminded him that in the modern wired world it was already out there, and anything Kevin said would more or less be damage control.

"Look, the first thing you need to understand is that the public perception of sharks is mostly wrong. Most of the species aren't going to look at a human and see a meal. There are a few, yes, and those will attack, but otherwise that's a completely wrong view perpetuated by *Jaws* and... am I allowed to say the name of the network that does the shark event every year?"

Vandergraf laughed. "They're competitors of the network we're working for, so don't say their name but feel free to smack talk them all you want. I know a few executives who will get a kick out of it."

"Um, yes, well, hammerheads are just one of the many species of shark that would rather mind their own business than attack a human, as long as the human isn't being threatening or there's blood in the water. I've seen one or two people just swim up to one and pet it. Although that wasn't here, though. There weren't enough sharks here to do that anymore, the way they'd been overfished. I was afraid for a long time that designating El Bajo as protected was a gesture that came too late."

"You seem to be talking in the past tense," Vandergraf said.

"That's because one week ago, uh, the sharks came back."

Vandergraf paused as though he hadn't heard that correctly. "They... came back? I knew there was an attack, but when you say they came back..."

"They came back. All of them. As in, one day hammerheads at El Bajo are a thing of the past, the next day there's hundreds of them."

"Wait, hundreds?"

"It's as if no one had ever hunted them," Maria said.

"Is that supposed to happen?" Vandergraf asked.

"If this were earlier in the year, I might almost say yes," Kevin said. "At their peak, it wasn't uncommon for the hammerheads to migrate spectacular distances and then return here to mate. But this is the wrong season. Their sudden appearance completely defies everything we thought we knew about their patterns."

"And that's not the only thing they're doing differently, am I right?" Vandergraf asked. "According to the news report…"

Kevin sighed. "Yes, the first two people who discovered the hammerheads had returned were attacked."

"Pretty viciously, too, if the reports in the media are to be believed."

"Come on, you're a reality show producer," Maria said. "You should know better than most how easy it is to manipulate a narrative." Vandergraf raised an eyebrow at her while Kevin shot her a look that clearly said *What the hell are you doing?* Maria winced and resolved to keep her mouth shut. She was the one who had convinced Kevin this whole thing was a good idea, after all. It probably wouldn't do to look antagonistic in front of the producer.

"What she means is the story got exaggerated and blown out of proportion," Kevin said. To Maria's ears, it sounded like a blatant lie that anyone would see through, but she might have just thought that because she was fully aware that it really was. Two local men had been out in a boat at twilight scouting for what they hoped would be a thriving marine tourist business now that El Bajo was protected. One had been in the boat while the other had been snorkeling. According to their reports, the water had been calm and empty. Then the snorkeler had come to the surface, screaming and bloody and desperate to get back in the boat. When the other man had pulled him in, he'd discovered bite wounds on both the snorkeler's torso and leg. Only seconds later, with blood swirling in the water, the surface was suddenly penetrated by, according to him, over twenty dorsal fins. That number had seemed unlikely until Maria had gone out to do a quick, unofficial survey and found that the initial reports were low. She counted nearly fifty hammerhead sharks close enough to the surface for her to see them unaided. There was no telling how many more were below swimming around El Bajo, and all alone in her Zodiac raft she hadn't dared don her scuba gear and check.

The snorkeler who had been attacked died from his wounds at the hospital. His partner had been telling the story to anyone who would listen ever since.

"So this is what we're going to be doing today? Stopping this captain and swimming with the sharks?" Vandergraf asked.

"Oh, there's not going to be any swimming involved," Kevin said.

"But I saw your volunteers loading wetsuits and scuba tanks."

"Standard equipment on the *Cameron* in case of emergencies," Kevin said. "All we're going to do is block the *Tetsuo Maru*'s way. Hopefully you can get something good you can use for the pitch reel, and if we have enough time left in the day we might even be able to tag a few hammerheads for our preliminary studies. It shouldn't be too eventful."

"So no piracy of the *Tetsuo Maru*?" Vandergraf asked with a wry smile.

Kevin shook his head. "Nothing so dramatic. It shouldn't be that big of a day."

Maria frowned at him but said nothing. He'd seen enough movies that he should have known better than to say that.

4

As Gutierrez continued to pilot the *Cameron* to El Bajo and their inevitable meeting with the *Tetsuo Maru*, Kevin took Vandergraf and the cameraman to get some footage of their research space below deck. Maria, in the meantime, called up all the One Planet volunteers to the deck and explained to them exactly what should happen at El Bajo and what they would be expected to do. As an organization, One Planet could be nebulous and flexible so she wanted to make sure there was no confusion about how to handle themselves. Founded by one of Kevin's colleagues about fifteen years ago, the idea was to create a sort of halfway point between citizen scientists and environmental activists. Kevin liked to use some of them from time to time when he needed extra hands that didn't need too much special training. There were actually many environmental groups that would have jumped at the chance to work with him, but Kevin had been dissatisfied and upset with the direction some of them had been going in recent years. Despite working with them earlier in his career, Kevin had even cut ties with Greenpeace entirely after they'd pulled a stunt at the Nazca Lines that had permanently damaged them. While Maria herself didn't have that same prejudice against Greenpeace, she was perfectly happy with working with One Planet instead. She'd started off as one of them, after all, and she felt they had the perfect combination of idealism and practicality.

Or at least they usually did. While the Gutsdorf siblings and Monica Boleau stood at attention as Maria went over safety precautions, Kirk Murphy and Diane Mercer were continuing to whisper to each other. At this point, Maria was deeply regretting letting them be a part of this trip. Had there been other volunteers available she would have made up some excuse why she didn't need them, but as it was they needed every single person on the Cameron short of Vandergraf and his cameraman to play a part in this.

"So here's how it's going to work," Maria said as she snapped her fingers in front of Murphy and Mercer to get their attention. "Normally for this sort of blockade action, we would prefer to have more boats, but today shouldn't really require much of a show of force. We just need to stop the *Tetsuo Maru* from doing anything for an hour or so. We'll have authorities coming to aid us after that. And besides, no one actually expects Captain Ito to be so blatant as to fish for sharks in illegal waters right in front of witnesses. To be completely honest, today is just about grandstanding for both our sides. They show us their disapproval at Westerners bullying them, we show them the law is on our side, and it should all break up peacefully."

"But how can you know that for sure?" Simon Gutsdorf asked. While his sister still looked resolute, he looked like he was second guessing his reason for being here.

"Look, there's nothing to worry about. I've been a part of these sorts of blockades before. As long as we did everything by the rule of law then nothing ever went sour. It'll all be fine."

"Why didn't we just alert the authorities the moment we found out the *Tetsuo Maru* was on its way?" Boleau asked. "That seems like the smartest plan of action, doesn't it?"

Maria tried not to show any outward sign of doubt. They hadn't alerted anyone because she had insisted they not, at least not until they were between the *Tetsuo Maru* and the El Bajo protected area. Her thinking had been that it would make a better impression with the producer if they looked like the heroes here. Kevin hadn't liked that, just like he hadn't liked getting in front of the camera in the first place. Now though she was beginning to have the smallest doubts about Vandergraf and the way he would present things. This possible show might not be worth the risk of not having a bigger authority backing them up, no matter how small that risk might be.

It wouldn't do any good to let the others see that she was having second thoughts, though.

"Just trust me, nothing we do or see today is going to be so dire that we'll actually need the *Armada de Mexico* to intervene. They'll just show up when we need the extra show of force. Now, I know we went over the basics last night but here's the whole plan."

Maria had brought a map with her clipboard. She knelt down on the deck to spread it out where everyone could clearly see it. It showed the lowest portion of the Sea of Cortez. She'd already marked everything she needed in black and red marker.

"This whole area here is obviously the El Bajo marine protected area," she said, indicating the rough black circle that matched the one on Kevin's larger map back home. In was in the sea between the Mexican states of California Baja Sur and Sinaloa, with the nearest land masses being the islands of Isla Partida and Isla Espirito Santo. Once they were in position, the two islands would be within visual distance, although not anything they could consider close. They would just be tiny spots on the horizon.

"We were prepared for the *Tetsuo Maru* to come from a variety of directions, but our eyes in the water indicated that they will be coming in from here." She pointed to the east of the two islands and El Bajo. "So that's where the *Cameron* is going to be waiting. We'll probably be the only boat in the area, since the local government has severely limited the number of tourist boats there since last week's incident. From our position here..." She indicated a specific point on the edge of the circle. "...we'll be able to see the *Tetsuo Maru* coming. At that point, Gutierrez will maneuver us into a good position and we'll put the two Zodiac rafts in the water. Monica, you'll stay behind and help with anything we might need to do in a hurry on the *Cameron*. Simon and Kirk, you'll be in Raft One to come up on the *Tetsuo Maru*'s leeward side. Diane and Cindy, you're Raft Two and will be to the windward side."

Diane tentatively raised her hand. *Good God, this isn't a fricking school*, Maria thought. "Yes Diane, what is it?"

"I don't know what leeward and windward means."

Oh dear lord, help me now, Maria thought. *I'm commanding someone who doesn't even know basic nautical terms*. Boleau looked equally disgusted while the Gutdorfs were obviously having trouble not laughing.

"Look, if the *Tetsuo Maru* is here and the *Cameron* is here," she said, pointing at two spots on the map, "then you and Cindy will go to this position while Raft One goes here. Got it?"

"Yes," Diane said. She didn't look at all like she did. Maria glanced in Cindy's direction, who nodded almost imperceptibly as if to say *Don't worry, everything will go according to plan.*

"Uh, Miss Quintero?" Murphy's hand started to creep into the air.

"Guys, you really don't need to do that," Maria said.

"Oh. Uh..." Murphy lowered his hand. "Can't I be on the same raft as Diane?"

Shoot me. Just shoot me now, please, Maria thought. She could think of no idea more disastrous than to put those two in one Zodiac together. "No, I made the assignments in a way I thought would be best for everyone."

Despite Maria's earlier admonition, Diane raised her hand again. At least this time she didn't wait to talk. "I really think me and Kirk should go together."

What the hell were they planning on doing, getting some quality make-out time in while a ship bore down on them? "I said no." Maria had trouble keeping the growing anger out of her voice. "People, I know I keep saying this is relatively low risk and mostly for show, except there's still a danger here. All we're going to do is form a short line that they won't be able to get around, and if they move we'll move too. But there's still a chance they could hit you on accident. Or even on purpose, although Ito has never struck me as that kind of person. Trust me, if the hammerheads are still as aggressive as they were last week then you don't want to end up in the water."

That finally appeared to seep into Mercer's thick head, considering she dropped her head and looked away. Murphy, on the other hand, looked like he was going to continue arguing the point until Cindy Gutsdorf thankfully interrupted him. "So what are the safety procedures then if we somehow end up in the water?"

Maria made sure to check that Vandergraf wasn't coming back up before she replied. She didn't exactly want to hide anything, but she didn't want him to have any more fuel for the fire either when it came to misrepresenting sharks. Once today was over, they could all finally get back to an honest study of whatever weird event was happening here. They even had all the equipment below already for their real studies. If they were lucky, they might soon be able to identify what was causing the hammerheads' strange behavior or even fix it.

"If you can, get back into the Zodiac as quick as you can. If for some reason you can't, the first step is not to panic. You'll all be wearing life vests so obviously you won't drown. If one of the sharks starts coming for you, remember that it's much more practiced than you at swimming so don't even try to turn around and get away. Normally, most sharks are more afraid of you than you are of them so kicking and splashing around will hopefully keep them away. If that doesn't work then you need to do your best to attack first. If it's right near the surface you can hit them on the snout right in the middle of their hammer-shaped head. However, if the shark is farther below the surface, the water resistance will make punching ineffective. As a last resort – and do remember that we're trying to protect them here so I do mean last, like they're going to take a bite out of you – then go for their eyes. No matter how endangered they are, if it's your life versus theirs then fight for your own first. Do not try to be a hero. With all that said, we're not expecting anything like that at all. Are there any other questions?"

She almost expected either Murphy or Mercer to do or say something else stupid. Thankfully, both of them kept their mouths shut, although Maria didn't miss the quick look they gave each other. She wasn't sure what that meant, nor did she particularly care at this point. All she could hope for at this point was that neither of them did anything stupid to screw this up.

"Okay then. Both of the raft teams, better do a final check of your equipment. Monica, go ahead and see if Gutierrez needs anything from you. If anyone needs me, I'll be right here."

They all left her alone. Maria let out a deep, long sigh. This wasn't exactly what she had signed up for when she'd started life with Kevin, but it would all be valuable experience once she got her own degree and was able to do the science on the same level. Until then, she would just have to use the little moments between to keep her sanity.

It was with that idea firmly in mind that she rested on the guard rails and stared out over the water, taking in the endless beauty, waiting for her first glimpse of the day of the sharks of El Bajo.

5

Maria didn't have to wait long. The *Cameron* had already gone around Isla Espirito Santo by the time she'd finished briefing the volunteers, which meant that they were on the edge of the El Bajo protected area. Kevin had instructed Gutierrez not to go straight through for fear that a fast moving boat might further disrupt whatever odd event was currently going on. Maria didn't have nearly the encyclopedic knowledge of sharks that Kevin did, but she knew enough to guess that if they were here in such force, it had to be because of something to do with mating, whether this fit their typical mating pattern or not. And if it was indeed all about hot shark action then the last thing they wanted to do was interrupt it and do potential harm to an already struggling population. So instead they skirted the edges. At this distance, it had been entirely possible that no would see any sharks at all. Except they did see them, and Maria had the privilege of being the first.

She'd made sure to have a pair of binoculars handy, and at the first sight of what might have been a dorsal fin slicing through the water she eagerly brought them up to her eyes. Sure enough she caught a brief glimpse of a fin just before it disappeared back below the water. That, she figured, would probably be the last anyone saw of them. However, a few seconds later she saw another come up, cruise around the surface for a little bit, and then go back down. And there was another, and then two at once. She adjusted the binoculars, trying to get an idea of what else might be so close to the surface that would draw so many of them there at once. If this was about mating then there shouldn't have been that many near the surface at all unless to feed. They should instead be deeper down, endlessly circling the undersea mount in their peculiar ballet. Instead, she continued to see more and more. None of them came anywhere close to the Cameron just yet, but at this rate she wouldn't be surprised if that was in the cards for the near future.

"See anything interesting?" Kevin said from behind. Maria

jumped, startled so much by his sudden appearance that if the strap for the binoculars hadn't been around her neck she probably would have dropped them into the sea.

"Sorry. Didn't mean to do that," he said, giving her an affectionate rub of the shoulder. She delighted at the touch until she realized they weren't alone. Vandergraf and his ever-present cameraman were right behind them, probably catching this entire intimate moment for later exploitation. Maria did her best not to show any outward annoyance, but after the antics of Murphy and Mercer she found it hard.

"Yeah, I do see something interesting. Take a look." She handed him the binoculars and let him take in the sight for himself.

"Huh," he said once he put the binoculars down. "That is strange."

"Gary, can you get that?" Vandergraf asked the cameraman.

"Sorry, too far away," Gary said. "Wouldn't show up well and I don't have the right lenses for that kind of shot. If we had a full crew with full equipment, then maybe."

"Full crew?" Maria asked. "How many more people would you actually need if this were a complete production?"

"More than we can probably fit on this thing," Vandergraf said. "If my bosses decide to pick this up then we'll have to get a different boat."

"You can't just get rid of the *Cameron*. It's part of the package." She noticed as she said this that the camera had come back around to her again.

"Don't get me wrong, it's great. Really fancy, totally impressive. It would make good television. But I think we can do more than that. I think we can make *great* television. And to do that we might need a bigger boat, one that wasn't named after the director of *Terminator*."

"Who also happens to be one of the very small number of people who've made it to the bottom of the Mariana Trench. Pardon me if I think that's something worthy of recognition."

"You know, I wanted to get a quick interview with you before all the action begins. Would you mind?"

That mollified her a little bit, but she still kept her guard up. "Oh. Uh, sure." This, she figured, would be a time to talk about what had drawn her to marine biology to start with. It might even make other people interested. That was, after all, why she had convinced Kevin to do this in the first place.

"Okay, good," Vandergraf said. He looked over his shoulder to see that Kevin was now out of earshot as he'd moved to another position in the hopes of getting a better glimpse of the sharks. "To start with, why don't you tell the viewers what it's like sleeping with someone as famous as Kevin Hoyt?"

Maria paused for several seconds. There was no way she could have heard that question coming from his mouth. It took her several breaths before she could admit that no, she had indeed heard him right.

"Excuse me?"

"I'm sure that sounds crass, but if you could just answer it. I'm starting to see a clear narrative here that I can edit together and sell to the network. Dr. Hoyt is the brains and you're the heart. Where's he's a cool customer, you're the passionate one. So give us some passionate details, something to really sell your character."

"I'm not just a fricking character on television. I'm a person."

"Come on, we don't need a lot. Just a few sound bites. I'm sure one of the biggest questions viewers will have is how someone like you can be intimate with…" He paused as though watching his language. "…someone like him."

"What the hell do you even mean, someone like me and someone like him?"

"You're young, passionate, very pretty. And he's, well…"

Maria had a sickening feeling that she knew exactly what point he was getting at. "Go on. Say it. Say what you want to say."

"Well, a him that wasn't always a him. You know, someone who used to be a woman."

It took every piece of her soul to remember that if she knocked him overboard and he was eaten by sharks the rest of the world would probably have an issue with that, no matter how supremely much he deserved it.

"Turn the camera off," she said. It surprised her how calm she actually sounded.

"What?" Vandergraf asked. "No. We can't…"

"Turn the camera off and I'll give you an answer. You can quote me on it later, if you want."

Vandergraf hesitantly waved for Gary to lower the camera. Once Maria was sure there wouldn't be any record of this, her hand shot for him and grabbed him by the crotch. Vandergraf made a funny little yipping sound. Gary just looked shocked. He also looked back down at his camera, obviously upset that it was missing this.

"Now listen here, you fucking pussbag," Maria said, still as calmly as though she were discussing the weather. "The fact that Kevin is transgender has nothing to do with anything. What we do together in private moments is none of your business. And if I catch you asking anyone else on the *Cameron* to speculate on what may or may not be between his legs, then I will make sure you no longer have anything between yours. Understood?"

She didn't wait for an answer. She just gave his squishy bits one more good hard squeeze, then let go and backed away. Vandergraf looked for a moment like he was going to collapse to his knees. Instead he leaned on the railing and got his balance back.

"I'll cut you out," he wheezed. "You're not going to be in this at all. You won't be in the demo reel, and when this becomes a full show you'll be edited out completely."

It was funny that he honestly believed that was the worst thing he could do to her. She had to wonder who he was in the rest of his life that the threat of not being on television was the most terrible thing he could imagine.

"Good luck with that," she said, then walked away to join Kevin watching the sharks. Some of the dorsal fins were closer now, and Maria hoped that he'd been so enraptured by this that he'd completely missed what had been going on just twenty feet behind him.

"That probably wasn't the smartest move," Kevin said quietly, his eyes never leaving the binoculars.

Maria sighed. "Sorry. I lost my cool."

"He could technically make the argument that that was sexual assault, you know. You could end up in court over that."

"You really think he's the kind of person who would do that?"

"No, not really. I am starting to think he's a douche though."

Maria suppressed a laugh. Kevin finally lowered the binoculars and flashed her a smile, but it disappeared quickly.

"What?" she asked.

"I can fight my own battles, Maria. I don't need you assaulting everyone who talks insensitively about me because I'm transgender."

"I… I'm sorry. He made me see red."

Kevin looked away. "Thank you, though."

Maria nodded.

After several seconds of awkward silence he offered her the binoculars. "Want one more look?"

"Nah, we're probably not going to see anything that answers the mystery on this trip. Wait…" Something on the horizon caught her eye, a small and distinctly unnatural shape. She took the binoculars before he could see it himself and used them to look.

It was a ship, and even at this distance she could identify it as one she had definitely seen before: the *Tetsuo Maru*. "There it is." She handed the binoculars back and then headed for the stairs below deck.

"Everyone get to your stations," she called out. "It's showtime."

6

The *Tetsuo Maru* was hardly the largest Japanese shark fishing vessel Maria had ever seen. In fact, given how much smaller it was than its brethren, she wouldn't have thought it was any danger at all to the shark population. But Kevin had shown her aerial pictures snapped of it after it had taken its share, and those images were brutal. Every available space on the deck of the ship had been occupied by bloody shark fins drying in the sun, the deck beneath them running completely red. The Tetsuo Maru could probably hold over a thousand fins in this manner and frequently did. Considering most of the largest shark groups Maria had ever heard of were in the hundreds, that was a lot of shark communities wiped out in just one voyage.

No matter its size compared to others like it, the *Tetsuo Maru* still looked intimidatingly large compared to the *Cameron*. It was twice as high and three times as long, and if Captain Ito had wanted to he probably could have rammed the *Cameron* easily and not experience anything more than minor damage to its hull. The *Tetsuo Maru* had been designed for long distance heavy-duty work, after all, while the *Cameron* had originally been designed for rich white men to compensate for small penises.

It was lucky for them, then, that Captain Ito didn't want to do any such thing. While Kevin might have been content to think the worst of the man, Maria had taken the time and effort to find out more about him. First off, he didn't strike her as the kind of person willing to risk the major international incident that would be caused by blatantly running over a world-famous marine biologist. Furthermore, he probably would have found any possible loss of human life appalling. Maria had found numerous references to him giving his time and money to charity. While the lives of endangered animals might have meant nothing to him, he didn't seem to have the same disregard for people.

"Okay, you guys know the drill!" Maria yelled. She noticed that, despite Vandergraf's threat earlier, Gary was making sure to record her every movement as she commanded the volunteers. "Exactly like we planned and everything will be smooth, got it?"

There were cries of "Yes" and "Got it" and even an "Aye aye," from one of the women. They all waited at the back of the *Cameron*, right at that spot where they would have launched a submersible if this had been a deep sea operation, as she inflated the first Zodiac. The volunteers all put on life vests. The Gutsdorfs even had wetsuits. She didn't anticipate anyone ending up in the water but she knew from experience that it could get cold in civilian clothes while out on one of the rafts. The spray from the ocean as the Zodiacs sped over the water could drop a person's body temperature fast, no matter how hot the sun might feel above. It probably would have been a good idea if Murphy and Mercer were wearing wetsuits as well. It was too late to tell them to change, though. The *Tetsuo Maru* was quicker than it looked, and they had to get into position now if they didn't want the ship to get past them.

Once the Zodiac was ready, she turned to look at the others. Boleau and Gutierrez were taking care of the boat while everyone else was on the deck watching her. Even Kevin had ceded control for the moment. He was all about the science. According to him he'd never been comfortable ordering people about.

"Double check to make sure everyone has their equipment." For this particular assignment, the equipment was minimal. Each raft would have two walkie-talkies and two non-lethal prods to use against the sharks if they absolutely had to. If they'd been dealing with something smaller, they would have also had bullhorns to talk to the ship. Instead the bullhorns were stored below and all attempts at communicating with the *Tetsuo Maru* would be from the bridge. Cindy took the two walkies for her Zodiac and double-checked the batteries. "I'm having problems with one of these."

"Here, let me see," Maria said. She walked over to Cindy and fiddled with the walkie. Everyone else watched, or at least she thought they all were until she heard something hit the water and a motor start up. She turned back to look at the Zodiac.

"Oh you've got to be kidding me," she said. Both Mercer and Murphy had jumped in and they were even now speeding away.

"Hey, get the hell back here!" Kevin yelled, but they either didn't hear him or didn't care.

"What are they even doing?" Simon asked.

"I have no idea," Maria said. She fumbled around until she found the binoculars.

"They didn't even take their gear," Cindy said, pointing at the deck. She was right. There were still four prods and two walkies on the deck.

"Stupid fucking idiots!" Maria mumbled. She looked at them through the binoculars and saw something she hadn't noticed in the previous couple minutes. They might not have the gear that had been assigned to them, but Mercer did have a backpack hanging from her shoulders. Whatever was in it, the pack looked stuffed to the point of almost busting its zippers.

"Well, they have equipment of some kind," she said to the others as she lowered the binoculars.

"So what are we going to do?" Cindy asked. Maria looked to Kevin, hoping he might have some insight. He looked completely bewildered himself. The only people who didn't appear to be confused by this turn of events were Gary and Vandergraf, Gary because she couldn't see his face from behind the camera and Vandergraf because he was desperately trying not to smile.

"Why would they do this?" Kevin asked.

"They wanted to be on a Zodiac together even when I said no," Maria said. "I have no idea why."

"Will they still do what we told them to do?"

Maria shrugged before looking at the Zodiac again through the binoculars. To her surprise, Murphy was piloting the raft with no problem. They looked like they were taking up one of the positions she'd ordered during the briefing.

"They look like they intend to," Maria said. "But without walkie-talkies we won't be able to give them orders if we have to change positions."

"We can go out to them and give them their equipment before we get into our position," Cindy said.

Maria looked at the *Tetsuo Maru*, getting ever closer with each second they spent trying to get their act together. *No more volunteers*, Maria thought to herself. *I've got to convince Kevin to hire professionals from now on.*

Kevin was the one who said what she was thinking. "There's no time. We have to do this now or they'll just zoom right past us and take up a spot over El Bajo."

Maria nodded in the direction of the Gutsdorfs. "You heard the man. Inflate the other Zodiac and get into position immediately. We're just going to have to cross our fingers that those two don't do anything else stupid."

Kevin walked briskly off in the direction of the bridge. His was the name Ito would recognize when Kevin called him over the radio, so he had to be the one to do all the talking. He even spoke a little Japanese. He wasn't fluent enough to hold a complete conversation but he knew at least how to get the captain's attention. He'd done it before after all. Kevin would also be the one directing Gutierrez to the most optimal positions.

While Kevin did that, Maria finished supervising the inflation of the remaining Zodiac, then stayed on the deck once the Gutsdorfs were off. Her job here was to keep an eye on the two rafts and act as the coordinator between them and the *Cameron*. She was happy to note that she finally had the deck all to herself. Gary and Vandergraf had followed Kevin, believing that would be where they would get the most interesting footage. If they had stayed here with her, Maria wasn't sure she'd be able to keep her temper if Vandergraf did or said something disrespectful again.

"Maria, this is Kevin checking in," her walkie-talkie squawked.

"I'm hearing you. Cindy and Simon, you hearing all this as well?"

"We're hearing you both just fine. Almost into position. How are we looking?"

"Everything looks okay so far." Indeed, at the moment everything looked like it was going exactly according to plan despite the hiccup regarding Murphy and Mercer. The *Cameron* stopped in a position directly between the *Tetsuo Maru* and the boundary marking El Bajo Marine Protected Zone. The Japanese ship also looked like it was slowly coming to a stop. On the bridge, Kevin would currently be going through his typical spiel, addressing a message to Captain Ito that his ship was currently in violation of local laws and blah, blah, blah. There might be some back and forth between Ito and Kevin, and there would almost certainly be a point where the *Tetsuo Maru* would test their resolve and play chicken with them. In the end they would go on their way before the Mexican Navy could arrive, though, and the *Cameron* would be the winner for this round. It was dance Maria had seen before. Okay, so it wasn't really piracy in any true sense, but she still enjoyed the feel like maybe there was at least a little danger involved.

Maria clipped the walkie-talkie to her belt and raised the binoculars. All the watercraft were exactly where she'd expected them to be, so she instead let her attention slip back to the sharks. There seemed to be even more dorsal fins than before, and although they all kept their distance from the *Cameron* and the Zodiacs, she couldn't help to think their movements were getting increasingly agitated. Something was spooking them, but she wasn't sure that it was the presence of the *Cameron* and *Tetsuo Maru*. All the activity seemed to be centered around a specific location, and that location was not, in fact, El Bajo like it should have been. Instead the center of the frothing mass of sharks appeared to be moving. Was it heading for one of the Zodiacs or was that just her imagination? She was just about to get on the walkie and warn them when she remembered that wouldn't do any good. The raft the sharks seemed to be inching toward was Murphy and Mercer's.

"Crap," she muttered. She pointed the binoculars in the direction of their Zodiac, hoping that one of them might be facing her direction so she could possibly flag them down or point out the bizarre shark behavior headed right for them. They probably weren't in any danger, but given how little they all knew about the behavior to begin with, she figured it was important they were at least aware. Neither of them were looking in her direction, however. Instead, both of them were staring intently at something on the floor of the raft with them. The pack was no longer on Mercer's back, so maybe it was something she'd been carrying. It was hard to tell from this distance, but they even looked like they might be having an argument over it.

"None of this feels right," she muttered to herself, then unclipped the walkie-talkie. "Kevin, how's it going in there?"

He didn't answer for about twenty seconds. "Ito is talking his usual smack about how we don't have right to do this and so forth and so on. Why? Is there something the matter?"

"Maybe. I want permission to move around the Zodiacs."

"If you think it can be done quickly. I don't want Ito to think we're leaving a hole open that he can get through."

"Roger that. Cindy, did you get that?"

"Yeah, but I'm not sure what it is you want us to do."

"I think Murphy and Mercer might be about to need your help. Wait. Hold on a second." Maria looked through the binoculars again at the young couple. Murphy was at the back of the raft again looking like he was about to move the Zodiac. She thought for a second that he had seen the sharks, except not once did he look behind him as the dorsal fins sliced ever closer. Mercer was still messing around with whatever was in the bottom of the raft. As Murphy started their motor going and pointed them in the direction of the *Tetsuo Maru*, Mercer finally sat back up with something in her hand. Maria tried to zoom in closer to get a look at it, but what she saw was so improbable that her mind didn't recognize it at first. She saw the silver color and the knobs at either end. There was also something strapped to it that might have been a cell phone.

Finally, Maria's mind caught up to her eyes. She hadn't understood at first because she'd never seen one in the real world, but she'd seen enough movies that she could recognize it for what it was meant to be.

Mercer was carrying a pipe bomb.

7

"A what?" Kevin yelled it loud enough that Maria wouldn't have needed the walkie-talkie. She could hear him on the bridge from here.

"A pipe bomb! Or something similar, I don't know. You've got to warn the *Tetsuo Maru*!"

Kevin didn't immediately reply. Marie suspected that, even if it was just for a second, he was considering letting Mercer do whatever she was going to do. Captain Ito was violating international law, after all, and he wouldn't have any grounds for protest if the *Tetsuo Maru* took any damage during such an action. There was even precedent elsewhere in the world, such as with the tactics of the Sea Shepherd organization and how they handled whaling vessels. But Sea Shepherd's tactics, while ethically suspect, were never intended to actually kill or hurt another human. They just wanted to make their point.

And Sea Shepherd sure as hell never used bombs. If that was indeed what Diane Mercer had out there, she and Murphy had crossed a very major line.

"Okay, radioing the *Tetsuo Maru* with a warning," Kevin finally said. "You get the Gutsdorfs to see if they can get to the other Zodiac and stop them. I'll have Gutierrez see what he can do about getting between their Zodiac and the ship."

Maria made sure the Gutsdorfs had heard all that, and as the *Cameron* turned and started toward the rogue Zodiac as fast as it could, Maria once more watched all that she could through the binoculars. Although the *Cameron* moved fast and could cut through the waves easily, there was a reason they used the Zodiacs to do most of the maneuvering between fishing ships and their targets. The rafts were quicker than the *Cameron* under most circumstances, and Mercer and Murphy's Zodiac had a significant head start on them. The Gutsdorfs gunned their engine and made a beeline for Mercer and Murphy, but they must have noticed the other Zodiac coming for them and only went faster. Now that the

Cameron was turned to face all three of the other vessels on the water, Maria ran to the bridge where she would still be able to see what was going on yet talk to Kevin at the same time.

Gutierrez didn't seem to notice her presence, given how intent he was at pushing the *Cameron* to its limit, while Kevin was similarly occupied with the radio. Gary and Vandergraf certainly noticed her though. As soon as she entered, the camera swiveled onto her. She shoved past them, trying to forget they were even there, and joined Kevin.

Kevin yelled something Japanese into the receiver. He waited several seconds for a reply yet none came. Kevin yelled something else, then looked out the window at the approaching *Tetsuo Maru* with uncontrolled disgust.

"Well?" Maria asked.

"Ito's not responding. I'm telling him he and all of his crew might be in danger, but I don't think he's taking any of it seriously. I mean, look."

He pointed out the window. Even without the binoculars she could see that the ship had started moving again. Ito might not have understood what the Zodiacs were doing but he had perceived a hole opening up in their defenses. Unfortunately for him, that only put the ship closer to Mercer and Murphy.

"We're close enough that Simon is trying to yell at them," Cindy said from the walkie, "but either they can't hear us over the wind and waves or else they're just ignoring us."

Kevin was the one who spoke to them this time. "Can you confirm what Maria said? Do they actually have a bomb?"

There was a long pause where Maria felt like her heart wanted to stop. Then finally Cindy answered. "Uh, confirmed. I think."

"Well which is it?" Kevin asked. "Confirmed or not?"

Another pause, although much shorter this time. "Simon says confirmed. It sure as hell looks like a bomb to him."

"Fuck!" Kevin said. Only then did he look like he remembered the camera recording his every word and movement. "Vandergraf, maybe you should turn the camera off. This isn't exactly—"

Vandergraf barked a laugh. "You're kidding, right? Gary, no matter what you do, do not stop recording."

Kevin appeared to be about to lose what little cool he had left before Maria touched his arm and shook her head. This was certainly bad, and oh holy hell were they all in for a world of hurt if any of this footage got out, but now was not the time for that fight. People might be about to die, and all because Mercer and Murphy wanted to... well, Maria still wasn't sure what their plan was here, although she could make a guess. Whether it was just the two of them working alone or they were doing this at the behest of some much more rogue environmentalist group, it was evident they intended to use the bomb to sink the *Tetsuo Maru*. Apparently they felt that when it came to between the lives of illegal fishermen and that of endangered sharks, the sharks were more important.

The sharks. During the last couple minutes Maria had completely forgotten about them. "Kevin, something weird is happening out there. With the hammerheads, I mean."

Gutierrez finally spoke. "Really, Maria? Now is not the time for that."

Kevin, however, didn't dismiss her concerns right away. He looked right at her, waiting to see if she thought whatever she'd seen was really important right now. Gutierrez had done this before, acting like anything out of her mouth was inconsequential. Maria wasn't even sure if he knew he was doing it. She'd seen him do it with Boleau as well. And with any woman, really. But Kevin wouldn't. Just because he was a man didn't mean he didn't have intimate knowledge of what it was like to be treated like his opinion didn't matter based on his gender.

Maria was grateful for that, but in this particular instance she had to second guess herself. They were in a pretty damn tense and important situation right now. Some odd behavior on the part of the sharks could probably wait. Even if the way so many of them had made a beeline for just the one Zodiac had tripped all the warning signals in her head, she couldn't let that be a factor at the moment. Once they managed to stop Mercer and Murphy, then they would be able to turn their full scientific attention to the sharks' weird schooling behavior.

Maria shook her head. Kevin responded with a barely perceptible nod. She loved him for that. If she had decided the sharks were a pressing concern, he would have listened.

The *Tetsuo Maru* had started to cross the border into El Bajo Marine Protected Area at this point, and the *Cameron* was now fast approaching it from the side. As speedy as they were moving, though, the two Zodiacs were quicker. "Cindy, give us a report," Maria said into her walkie-talkie. "What's happening out there?"

"They're still outpacing us, but I don't know how long it would take them to put that bomb on the hull and get to a safe distance. We might be able to stop this."

As Kevin went back to yelling into the radio, now speaking completely in English as his limited Japanese was no longer enough to suitably warn Ito of what danger they were in, Maria lowered the walkie-talkie and thought about this. If this had really been Murphy and Mercer's plan all along, it was a stupid one. Cindy was right. They could reach the other Zodiac before Mercer had finished setting the bomb up, a process that would have been even harder considering the *Tetsuo Maru* was still moving at a speed that would challenge the Zodiac's tiny engine just to keep steady alongside it. Either the couple really were that dumb or else there was more to this plan than anyone else was seeing.

"Come on, you idiots," Maria muttered to herself. "You know we can stop you. Why would…"

A thought suddenly occurred to her. No. That couldn't be it. They wouldn't. Would they? It hadn't seemed to Maria that they were really so ruthless as to do something like that, but then she also hadn't thought they were the kind to use bombs to get a simple environmental point across either.

"Shit," she said, much louder this time.

Kevin stopped his frantic pleas to the *Tetsuo Maru*. The ship was slowing down, so maybe what he'd been saying was starting to get through to them. Of course, that also made them easier targets for the two maniacs in their raft.

"What is it?" Kevin asked.

Maria didn't answer him, instead turning to talk to Gutierrez. "Where the hell is Monica right now?"

"There was a crash in one of the labs like something had fallen over," Gutierrez said. "She went to go check on it. Why?"

Maria spoke into her walkie again. "Boleau, can you hear me?"

There was a pause before Boleau answered. "Yeah, what is it?"

"Are you anywhere near the engines?"

"Close enough. Why?"

"Get out of there. Get out of there now!"

Cindy's voice came through now. "Mercer has something else in her hands. It looks like… she has a walkie-talkie after all."

It wasn't a walkie-talkie, Maria realized. It was a remote.

"Monica, get away from the engines!" Maria screamed. It was loud enough that Boleau probably would have heard her even without the walkie-talkie. She didn't have any time to respond, however, because right then a sudden boom rocked the entire *Cameron*.

Those bastards.

"Holy shit, what was that?" Gutierrez asked. The *Cameron* suddenly slowed and both the Zodiacs continued zooming on toward the *Tetsuo Maru* without them. Maria didn't wait around long enough to answer. She ran out of the bridge and down the steep steps to below deck. Immediately at the bottom of the ladder was one of the small, cramped labs with multiple specimen tanks full of water. One had come loose and fell to the floor, leaving it soaked in salt water. That, however, didn't concern Maria just now. She was much more worried about the acrid scent of smoke in the air.

Monica was on the floor near the nearest door to the engine compartment, coughing as something thick and black wafted through the air. Maria stopped only long enough to stoop and make sure she was okay, no broken bones or abrasions or anything that suggested she'd been near the engine. Once she was satisfied, she continued on through the door, hoping against hope that she was wrong about what had just happened.

She wasn't wrong. The explosion had been small and controlled, only slightly scorching the walls and not doing any structural damage to the trimaran's hull. But the engines were devastated. Mercer had blown them up.

8

There wasn't any time to inspect the damage, and yet paradoxically they couldn't do anything else other than stand on the bridge and watch the rest of this morbid show play out.

Monica, once she'd stopped hacking up her lungs, had rooted around in their equipment and found another pair of binoculars. The two sets made their rounds between Maria, Kevin, Monica, and Gutierrez, each of them taking a few moments to see what was happening with the Zodiacs before passing them on to the next person. Gary and Vandergraf declined their turns. They were too busy watching the crew yell and scream and cry, all of it getting captured in Gary's camera.

Maria had yelled into her walkie to tell Cindy what had happened. Kevin had resumed his frantic warnings to the *Tetsuo Maru*. Cindy had stayed silent, although Maria hoped that was because they were too busy dealing with Mercer and Murphy and not because something was wrong with the signal. The *Tetsuo Maru*, however, had finally responded, even if it was just, according to Kevin, the Japanese version of saying they didn't believe him and he should fuck off. Despite that, the *Tetsuo Maru* had come to a full stop on the wrong side of El Bajo's border and a number of people could be seen on the deck staring down at the two approaching Zodiacs.

"What the hell are they doing?" Gutierrez asked. "When someone says there's a bomb approaching, you'd think they would, I don't know, at least grab some guns and fire some warning   shots."

"They probably don't have a lot of guns onboard," Maria said.

"Harpoons then," Gutierrez said.

Kevin shook his head. "They're so used to people like us that don't actually resort to violence, they don't believe anyone associated with us would do such a thing. They just think it's the next level of scare tactics."

"Well they're sure as hell about to be scared, all right," Maria said. She happened to be holding the binoculars right as Murphy pulled up next to the ship. As he tried to keep the Zodiac in place, Mercer immediately got to work attaching the bomb to the hull. Kevin relayed all of this to the Tetsuo Maru, and finally several of the crewmen on the deck pulled out harpoon guns and aimed them at the raft below them.

"Oh God," Monica said, handing her binoculars next to Gutierrez. "Oh God, I can't watch this."

Maria would have agreed that this was about to become a bloodbath, but Mercer appeared to realize what was going on and interrupted what she was doing long enough to reach back down into her pack in the raft. When she came back up she had a hand gun. She fired several shots into the air, aiming more in the crewmen's general direction rather than actually trying to hit any of them. They all scattered, only one of them managing to fire a harpoon before he ducked away. The harpoon went wild, ironically coming closer to hitting the Gutsdorfs as they tried to get within grabbing distance of the other Zodiac. Mercer handed the gun to Murphy, who pointed it at the Gutsdorfs and appeared to be shouting something at them. Both of the Gutsdorfs held up their hands where Murphy could see them while Mercer continued her work with the bomb.

"Seriously?" Gutierrez asked. "They seriously had a gun on them the whole time and none of us knew?"

Maria just gave an exasperated shrug. It wasn't like she'd ever had cause to frisk all the volunteers before a voyage before. "Kevin, you need to tell them they need to prepare some life rafts. The Gutsdorfs aren't going to be able to stop this. And then get on the channel for the Mexican Navy. We're probably going to need rescue operations."

"And they're going to need to arrest the shit out of Murphy and Mercer," Monica added.

"That too," Maria said, although she had to wonder if that would happen. So far those two had thought to disable their engines, had come armed, and apparently knew how to rig up bombs. None of that implied that they were doing any of this on impulse. They'd planned it, or if they really were as dumb as they had looked and it hadn't just been an act, then someone else had planned it for them. And with that level of planning there had to be an option for escape somewhere.

"Cindy, if you can hear this, get the hell out of there," Maria said into the walkie. "Not only do you not want to get shot, but unless you've spent some time in a bomb squad I doubt you'll be able to disarm it." Maria didn't think Mercer would have a bomb sophisticated enough that it would automatically explode if either of the Gutsdorfs messed with it, yet she wasn't going to underestimate them again.

Gutierrez had her binoculars by this time. "They're breaking off. Looks like they're trying to get their distance. And Mercer looks done."

Maria took the binoculars back from him. The Gutsdorfs were heading back to the *Cameron* as fast as their little raft could go. Mercer and Murphy were also putting some distance between themselves and their handiwork, although they were pointedly going in an entirely different direction than the *Cameron*. They couldn't possibly get far. The Zodiacs were great for going ashore somewhere remote or moving quickly, but they didn't carry that much fuel and Maria doubted that Mercer had any extra in her bag of tricks. The nearest land was Isla Partida, and after some quick calculating, Maria figured that if they made a beeline right for it they would come up just short enough for it to be a problem. However, they weren't even going in that direction. Instead they were heading deeper into the Sea of Cortez.

Whether they noticed it or not, they were also heading right for the enormous school of sharks. Maria didn't have any time to comment on that, though. That was when the bomb went off.

There was enough distance between the *Cameron* and the *Tetsuo Maru* that the explosion didn't sound terribly loud in Maria's ears. The flash, however, was bright enough that Maria had to look away for a second before putting her eyes back to the binoculars and trying to survey the damage. There was still too much smoke coming from where the bomb had been for her to see exactly how big of a hole it had made, but it was enough that the *Tetsuo Maru* immediately started to sink nose first.

"My God," Monica whispered. The entire rest of the bridge was quiet. Maria felt like they should be doing something, anything, and yet the *Cameron* could do nothing more than float along aimlessly as the current slowly took it in the direction of El Bajo. Maria looked around, hoping someone else might have an idea, but everyone was too stunned to even move. Even Vandergraf, previously looking like he was having the time of his life, now looked pale.

"Boss?" Gary asked quietly. "Should I, uh, stop filming? This doesn't feel right."

Vandergraf took a moment to think it over before he shook his head. "No. Keep filming. We'll need the evidence."

Maria turned to Kevin. "Honey? What should we do?"

"I... I'm clueless," he said. "This is so very far outside of my typical marine biology experience."

Maria took a deep breath. "Okay." Another breath. Time to take charge then. "Okay. Keep trying to reach the Navy. They shouldn't be too far from here by now, right?" She didn't stop to find out the answer. "Gutierrez and Boleau, get to the engines and see if there's anything you can do with them. Anything at all. Find us paddles if you have to."

The *Cameron* rocked beneath them as they were hit by a wave from the explosion. Several more dorsal fins popped up on the surface. The explosion had probably disturbed them right when a large number of people from the *Tetsuo Maru* were about to go in the water.

"What are you going to do while we're busting our ass?" Gutierrez asked. He tried to sound stand-offish even though Maria thought she heard a note of relief in his voice that someone was telling him what to do.

"I'm going to see what we can do about rescue," she said. "Gary, Vandergraf, you're following me."

Gary started to object. "We can probably get better shots of those two that did this if we—"

"Stop arguing and do what I say," she said. She left the bridge without looking behind her to make sure they followed.

She still had the binoculars with her when she came out on the deck. The *Cameron* had drifted enough at an angle that she was still able to get a good view of the *Tetsuo Maru* even from the back, and she looked that direction just long enough to confirm that there were people getting into life rafts and dropping them in the ocean. She couldn't exactly judge the speed that the ship was sinking, but she didn't think any of it would still be above the water two minutes from now. Not all the crew would make it into life rafts. What she needed to do was figure out how to keep the hammerheads from savaging those who went into the drink.

They had one more spare life raft, but unlike the Zodiacs it was designed purely for emergencies and didn't have their engines. It was better than nothing, and she immediately started inflating it. While she was doing this, she spoke to the Gutsdorfs. "Cindy, please tell me you guys are out there making a rescue effort."

"We've already got one guy out of the ocean. At most we can hold three or four more."

"Good. Keep those prods ready. The sharks are—"

"Holy hell," Gary said from behind her. Maria looked over her shoulder to see both him and Vandergraf staring gape-jawed out at the sea. Maria glanced in that direction, figuring they were just speechless at the sight of their first shipwreck, then did a double take. They weren't watching the *Tetsuo Maru* at all, as it was no longer the most spectacular sight in front of them.

Between them and the *Tetsuo Maru*, the ocean practically boiled with hammerhead dorsal fins. Had anyone else ever told her about this sight she would have thought they were exaggerating, but *boiled* was truly the only word that seemed to fit. The waters roiled and tossed at the sheer number of sharks. There were hundreds of them, all at the surface, probably more than had ever been at El Bajo prior to them being fished to near extinction. One or two even breached and flung themselves temporarily into the air, which was a practically unheard of behavior in this species.

"Oh my God, Maria are you seeing this?" Cindy asked.

"Move!" Maria said. "Get everyone you can out of the water right now. I don't know what this is, but you…"

She stopped mid-sentence. There was something else out there. Something huge.

Even with all the other sharks disturbing the water, she could still see the shadowy outline of something as it passed beneath the *Cameron*. From its size, her first thought was that it had to be some kind of whale. Her best guess was that it was somewhere between twenty-five and thirty feet long, making it longer than even a great white shark would have been. It couldn't have been a whale, though, given the activity of the hammerheads. Any nearby whales would be running for the hills.

She wondered for a moment if this was exactly the reason all those whales had been beaching this morning, although she didn't have the time to give it any further thought. As it got further away, Maria lost sight of the massive shape, yet she was still able to follow it by the way all the other sharks seemed to part ahead of it like a mass of people scrambling to let a dictator through lest he take undue notice of them.

Then something came up through the water. A dorsal fin, probably about as tall as Maria herself.

This was most definitely not a whale.

Suddenly the raft sitting on the deck next to Maria didn't feel like it would make a lick of difference.

"Oh God, the sharks are getting some of the fishers..." Cindy said. As horrible as that image was, Maria felt like they all had to move it they wanted to avoid one that was much worse.

"Cindy, get back to the *Cameron* now!" she screamed into the walkie-talkie.

"But there's still people in the water..."

"Something else is out there, and it's heading right for..." Maria stopped. She was going to say that it was heading for the Gutsdorfs and their measly attempt at a rescue operation. No sooner did she say it, though, that the fin made an abrupt turn and the vanished below the surface again. Instead of heading for the middle of the mass of hammerheads, it had looked like it was heading for the outer edge. Maria followed the last trajectory she had seen it on and found Mercer and Murphy, still moving away and apparently unaware of the bizarre carnage they'd left in their wake.

Maria would wonder later if, had the two traitors had their walkie-talkies with them, she would have warned them. She wanted to think of herself as a good enough person that she would have tried, but in the moment with so much chaos to blame on them she couldn't be certain. It was a moot point, though. There was no way to communicate with them. All she could do was stand on the deck and watch what was simultaneously the most majestic yet most horrific sight she had ever seen in her life.

The speed with which the giant form reached the Zodiac was remarkable. No sooner had it disappeared below the water than it came up again. And it didn't just come up to show its dorsal fin. It rose straight up out of the water head first as though in that brief period of time it had dived deep and then rocketed back up, surfacing directly underneath the Zodiac. The whole thing happened so fast that Maria was unable to get the binoculars to her face to see any details, although she had a clear vision in her mind of the startled and uncomprehending expressions on Mercer and Murphy's faces. In the first few milliseconds, all Maria could see of the creature was a wall of water rising up with it. The Zodiac was launched into the air where it comically seemed to hang for an unusual amount of time, the air in it and its shape causing it to drift back down to the water slowly like a parachute. Mercer and Murphy weren't so lucky. The two of them flew in the air, with Murphy actually pinwheeling his arms as though he thought that would give him better balance or maybe even help him fly. Mercer was ejected to the side and hit the water almost immediately. Ironically, despite all the sharks milling about, that was probably what saved her life.

The water fell away but the creature kept going up, finally giving Maria a clear view of it if only for the space of a heartbeat. The distinctive shape of the head made it very clear that this thing was a hammerhead shark, but the size of it was unlike anything she had ever thought possible for the species. In those few seconds she had to assess the shark, she guessed that her earlier estimate of its length was wrong. From nose to tail, this thing had to be around forty feet, comparable to a whale shark. Instead of the blue or gray color typical in most sharks this one had brown mottled skin. It also had its mouth wide open.

No one had a chance to scream or cry out or even try to look away. The shark's jaws closed on Murphy's hip, ripping him almost in half with just that one bite. Even from this distance, Maria could see his blood spurting and completely coating the shark's t-shaped head.

Then gravity finally took over again. The shark dropped back to the water at a slight sideward angle, causing an enormous splash that sent shockwaves through the teaming sharks. As though that was a cue they had been waiting for, all of the other sharks disappeared below the surface, the water becoming calm as they vanished. The enormous hammerhead's dorsal fin could still be seen above the water for a few more blinks before it dropped below the surface as well. The Zodiac hit the water last, and with that once again the ocean looked as it should be.

The entire incident, from the explosion in the *Cameron*'s engine room to the giant hammerhead vanishing, had only lasted about five minutes.

Maria stood frozen in place. She couldn't speak. What even could she say? From behind her, though, Vandergraf did not have the same problem.

"Gary, please tell me you got that on camera," he said quietly.

Maria turned to see Gary, just as shell-shocked as her, with the camera still up to his face. He lowered the camera and, without even closing his slack-jawed mouth, nodded that he had indeed.

9

"What the hell... *what the hell... WHAT THE HELL WAS THAT*?!"

Gutierrez's voice as he ran up next to her finally broke Maria out of her stupor. Monica followed close behind.

"What? What was it?" Monica asked. "I didn't see."

Maria didn't have the slightest clue how to answer that. And giving the colossal hammerhead a name or trying to study it was the last thing they needed to do on a very long list.

"We don't have time to talk about it," Maria said. "It might be back and we need to get as many people onto the *Cameron* as we possibly can before..." Except at the moment she wasn't sure what she thought would happen next. The hundreds of sharks and their one freakish relative had disappeared just as quickly as they appeared. That behavior made just as little sense as anything they had been doing before that. So she couldn't predict whether they were really gone or for how long. She just knew they needed to take advantage of this moment of relative peace for however long they had it.

She suddenly remembered that she still had the walkie-talkie in one hand and the binoculars in the other. "Cindy?" she asked the walkie. "Cindy, are you still there?"

There wasn't any response.

"Cindy, please tell me nothing happened to you guys."

For several seconds the silence continued. Then it was broken as the walkie-talkie squawked, "*Did you fucking see that?*"

"I saw. Continue with rescue operations and move it. Direct all the life rafts you see to get to the *Cameron*." She paused, still taking in what she had just seen. "Please hurry. It doesn't look like the Zodiac is going to be any kind of defense against that thing."

There was a sound that might have been Simon snatching the walkie from Cindy's hands. "Oh gee, you think?" There was a distinct note of manic panic in Simon's voice, but Maria could see their Zodiac as it started moving again.

"Gutierrez and Boleau, both of you get back to the engines now. We need to get the hell out of here yesterday."

"What?" Monica continued asking as Gutierrez pulled her back inside. "Would somebody please tell me what's out there?"

Gutierrez babbled on as they went in. It sounded like all he had seen was that last fleeting glimpse of the ridiculously large dorsal fin, but that was enough to scare the hell out of him.

"It's a fair question," Vandergraf asked. All signs of his earlier cockiness were gone, replaced by a grim, serious expression. "What is out there?"

Maria used the binoculars to see the place where the hammerhead had gone back below the water, then set them down on the deck. "Survivors. Come on, you two. We're going out there."

Just as she had suspected, neither of them moved. "Out, uh, out there?" Vandergraf asked.

"No, we're just going to rescue the people that are here on the deck. Of course out there."

"You did just see the same thing we did, right?" Gary asked. "If you somehow missed it, I can show you the footage again."

The thought of watching what had happened to Murphy again made her queasy. She hadn't liked the guy even before she had realized he was some kind of eco-terrorist, but that didn't mean she would have wished that fate on anyone. Which was exactly why she needed to talk some sense into these two and get out on the water fast.

"Whatever the hell caused all the sharks to act like that looks like it's stopped for now. I highly doubt it's going to stay that way for long. I'm going out there with or without you, but I'm going to have problems if I'm doing it just by myself. If there's still people in the water when the sharks come back and you could have done something to stop it, are either of you really going to be able to live with yourself?"

Gary was the first one to take a deep breath and nod his head. "Okay. What do you need me to do?"

"You can start by putting down that God-damned camera. If you try to take it with us, it's only going to get in the way." She looked at Vandergraf. "And you?"

It took him more time, but he eventually silently nodded as well.

Maria got a couple of oars and, with a lot of reluctance on everyone's part, the three of them got in the emergency life raft and pushed off from the *Cameron*. She kept in touch with the Gutsdorfs to make sure they were all right, but instead of going toward them and survivors of the *Tetsuo Maru* she pointed Vandergraf and Gary in the direction of Murphy and Mercer's Zodiac.

"Oh hell no," Gary said.

"Murphy may be dead but Mercer still seems to be alive. We can't just leave her floating out to sea."

"Now that the camera's not rolling I have no problem saying this," Vandergraf said, "but why the hell not? We may not know how many made it off the *Tetsuo Maru* yet but it probably wasn't the whole crew. Some of them probably drowned and others were killed by the sharks. She's a murderer."

She thought about taking the high road and saying that she didn't deserve this kind of fate or that she needed to be put in front of a jury for what she had done, except Maria wasn't sure she was willing to risk her life on the open water just for that. Instead her reasoning was much more pragmatic. "She's a murderer who had an escape plan. We need to know what it was just in case Gutierrez and Boleau can't fix the engines."

"But the Navy's coming, right?" Gary asked. "You said they were going to show up not long into the encounter with the *Tetsuo Maru* anyway, and Dr. Hoyt was trying to get them to come sooner."

"Maybe, but Mercer still might have information that's important. Especially since I don't think she and Murphy were working alone."

Vandergraf raised an eyebrow as he realized what she was getting at. "You don't think it's just us out here on the sea right now, do you?"

"They were headed farther out to sea. There's no way that makes any sense unless they were expecting someone to pick them up."

They rowed as fast as they could despite every dip of the oars in the water making Maria nervous. Given the timing, it seemed likely that the sharks and their gigantic friend had been agitated by the explosion and the sinking ship. For all she knew, every little disturbance on the surface could be telling the hammerheads that the raft was another suitable target. The closer they got to the abandoned Zodiac the more nervous Maria became. What would happen if the super-hammerhead decided to pop up right now? Would they get a warning or would its jaws crush all three of them before they even knew they were in trouble? Given the behavior she had seen from the *Cameron,* she thought they would at least see its dorsal fin, although that still wouldn't be ample warning given how fast it had been.

They could see Diane Mercer floating in the water for a full minute before they reached her. Given how still she was Maria was afraid the girl had died, possibly from the shock to her system or some wound that Maria hadn't been able to see with the binoculars. As they approached, though, Mercer began flailing like she had just now decided that she was going to drown despite the life vest that had kept her alive this far still firmly on her body.

"Stop flailing," Maria called out to her. "You might attract the sharks again."

Mercer immediately stopped moving. They were close enough now that Maria could clearly see the look of abject terror on her face. Maria tried not to take too much pleasure in that.

Once they were close enough she had Vandergraf and Gary help her haul Mercer into the raft. After she was in Gary "accidentally" smacked her in the head with his oar as he went to put it back in the water. He looked disappointed that she was already too dazed to notice or comment on it.

"Oh god," Mercer said through her quivering lips and chattering teeth. "Oh god, thank you. Thank you thank you thank you."

"You shut your damned mouth right now or I'm going to shut it for you," Maria said. Mercer looked taken aback by this and turned to the other two as though she expected them to come to her defense. Maria couldn't help but notice the way Vandergraf unconsciously brought his legs together tighter. He was probably happy that Maria's wrath was focused on someone else this time.

"So we've got her," Gary said. "Now what?"

"We'll want the Zodiac, too," she said. "From here it looks a little deflated, but it's not completely flat, so we still might be able to use if in a pinch. And then…" She looked back in the direction of where the *Tetsuo Maru* had once been. Large amounts of flotsam were bobbing in water but the ship itself had by now completely vanished into the sea. Most of the lifeboats looked like they were headed to the *Cameron* and Maria couldn't see any more people flailing their arms for help. Either they had drowned, been eaten, or rescued by now. There wasn't much else they could do out here.

"And then we grill this bitch," Maria finished. Mercer, already a bluish-pale from her time in the cold water, somehow managed to look even paler.

Maria directed them to start rowing for the Zodiac, yet she called for them to stop before they'd taken more than two strokes. Farther out she could see fins again.

"Oh shit," Vandergraf said. "They're going to come for us. They're going to—"

"Wait," Maria said, holding up her hand. Something about the sharks' movements looked different this time. When she'd first seen the fins pop up and head for Murphy and Mercer's Zodiac, there had been something undeniably predatory about the motions. This was different. She saw four dorsal fins cutting through the sea, yet they weren't in any kind of formation she'd ever seen. They sliced through the space between them and the Zodiac before vanishing back below. Maria got the impression that the others in the raft wanted her to give the okay for them to go forward again, but she didn't. She waited, starting to form an idea of what was going on and knowing that if she watched long enough it could be confirmed or denied. After about half a minute it was confirmed. Four more dorsal fins appeared right about where they'd first seen them. They went through the water between the two rafts and then vanished again.

"Go forward toward the Zodiac," Maria said quietly. "But do it slowly. Very, very slowly."

"I don't understand," Vandergraf said.

"I'm not one hundred percent certain I am either," Maria said. "But I've got a suspicion."

The three of them (since Mercer was still too shaky to be any help) dipped their paddles in the water and inched forward. At this rate it would take them forever to reach the Zodiac, but by now Maria suspected they weren't going to reach it one way or the other.

Again the four fins appeared. As the emergency raft got closer to them, the sharks swam in a more agitated manner, splashing the water as though in a show of force. No, Maria realized. Not just *as though*. Exactly like a show of force. It was a blatant attempt to scare them back. Hammerhead sharks shouldn't have been able to make that kind of intelligent decision. Then again, they shouldn't have been swimming single file in a patrol between them and the Zodiac. Because that was exactly what they were doing. The sharks were guarding them.

"Just keep moving," Maria said. "Maybe a little faster now. Let's see if—"

They didn't have time to see if anything. The water exploded in front of them as something enormous once more breached the surface. This time, however, it wasn't with quite the same showmanship that it had first attacked the Zodiac and killed Murphy. Maria only got the quickest glimpse of the shark's deep brown head as it came up and latched its teeth into the side of the Zodiac. When it went back down into the water, the resulting splash soaked all four of them in the emergency raft. Mercer and Gary both screamed, although Gary's could barely be heard next to Mercer's high-pitched, panicked squeak of pure fear. When the water settled, they could still see shredded parts of the Zodiac floating on the surface, but the engine and any hope of it every being intact enough for anyone to ever ride in it again were gone.

"Oh God oh God oh God," Mercer said. "It almost got us. It almost got us!"

"No," Maria said. "It didn't."

"Are you blind?" Vandergraf asked. Apparently in the heat of the moment all worry about damage to his balls was gone. "It was only like ten feet in front of us! We've got to get back to the *Cameron* before it comes back."

Maria nodded and directed them to immediately start rowing back to the *Cameron* at full speed (Mercer now joining them, having gotten over her shock enough that she rowed faster than all the others and tended to send them slightly off course). She knew full well that they didn't have anything to worry about, at least not in this exact moment, but she was afraid if she said so the others would think her crazy. Once back at the Cameron she would have to discuss this with Kevin to see if they could come up with some scientifically plausible explanation. For now though, she knew exactly what this had been. They were being directed to stay within a specific space. She didn't know how and she didn't know why, but that gigantic hammerhead was directing the other sharks to keep them in place.

It was intentionally imprisoning them alone out here on the sea.

10

To Maria's chagrin, she got back on the *Cameron* just in time to learn right along with everyone else that Simon had named the monster shark Teddy Bear.

"I told you earlier we weren't going to call it that," Cindy said. They'd gotten back to the Cameron ahead of everyone else, unloading the six people they'd been able to rescue before assisting survivors off the other lifeboats. Despite everything else that had just happened, this one little act of her brother seemed to offend her most of all.

"Teddy Bear?" Maria asked as she shoved Mercer up onto the deck, where she promptly collapsed into a crying mess that everyone else ignored for now. "The hell?"

Simon shrugged. "You know. Because it's brown."

"A lot of things are brown, not just teddy bears," Cindy said. "Real bears, dirt, shit..."

"Yes, by all means let's just call it Shit," Gutierrez said. He was using bandages from one of the first-aid kits to wrap up a head-wound on a dazed-looking sailor. "That name is going to be taken so much more seriously."

"We don't exactly have to name it anything," Kevin said as he came out on deck, gingerly stepping over the Japanese sailors sitting all over. There were far more people on the Cameron now than there safely should have been, but they didn't want to leave them in lifeboats in case Teddy Bear made another attack. "We could always just call it 'That One' and I'm pretty sure we'd all know which one we're talking about."

Maria perked up when she saw him. "Did you get a hold of the Mexican Navy? Are they almost here?"

Kevin sighed. "Yeah, about that. There's a problem."

"Oh come on. You've got to be kidding me," Maria said.

"According to the original schedule, they were supposed to be here no more than fifteen minutes from now. But most of the ships got diverted to investigate the whale beachings."

"What? They knew the *Tetsuo Maru* was on its way. Didn't they think that was more important?"

"That's what I said, and I got a bit of an ass-chewing by one of their higher ups. Apparently not everyone thinks protecting an endangered marine animal sanctuary is worthy of military intervention."

"And beached whales are?"

"No, I think someone just diverted them because they think we meddle too much and wanted to teach us a lesson. They were as shocked as us that this has resulted in the *Tetsuo Maru*'s sinking."

"So how long will it be before any of their ships can reach us?"

"An hour and a half at the earliest."

"An hour and a half," Maria said, looking out over the currently calm waters. There were still plenty of shadows moving just below the surface, though. "A whole hell of a lot can happen in an hour and a half. What about the engines?"

Gutierrez made a rude noise. "I don't think there's anything we can do. They're so shot that we'd have a better chance of moving if we slapped the outboard motors from the Zodiacs onto the back."

As ideas went, it might have sounded stupid, but the tiny bit of push they'd get that way might be better than nothing. However, if Maria's theory about Teddy Bear (and she hated that she was now thinking of the shark by that name) was correct, then any attempt at all at them leaving wouldn't result in them getting far.

Maria glanced around at the crew of the *Tetsuo Maru*. A few of the less injured ones were talking quietly to each other in Japanese, but on the whole they were subdued. Maria couldn't blame them, given what they had just been through. "Is Captain Ito here?" she asked.

Kevin said nothing for several seconds, only staring down at his feet. Without looking up he said, "A couple of people on the crew say he went down with the ship. He's certainly not here, at least. I've cursed his picture enough that I would recognize him."

Maria could tell that his emotions were complex right now. On the one hand the two of them had been nemeses, yet Kevin was not the kind to ever wish death on a person. There might even be a part of Kevin that blamed himself for this. The time for considering that would have to be later, though. Right now they needed to confront the one person in their company who was most responsible.

Mercer was sitting on the deck near the back, although Maria noticed that she had scooted a healthy distance from the water. Maybe she thought a shark could still jump up and snatch her if she got too close. While a number of the *Tetsuo Maru* crew members had emergency blankets wrapped around them, Mercer was forced to make do with just her own wet clothing. She shivered furiously and her lips might have been a slight shade of blue. It was almost enough for Maria to feel sorry for her. Almost.

"Mercer," Maria called. "Come with us. We're going to the bridge."

"W-w-w-why?" she asked. "I d-d-don't think I c-c-c-can move."

Maria got close enough that only Mercer would be able to hear her. "Because you're about to tell us everything we want to know. And if you don't, well, there are a large number of Japanese sailors around us right now who are probably too shell-shocked to realize you're the one who tried to kill them."

"What? That wasn't what we were trying..."

"It doesn't fucking matter what you were trying to do. All that matters is what you actually did. And how much revenge they might want if they find out you're the reason a bunch of their friends died."

Diane Mercer stared at her for several seconds as though she couldn't believe that anyone would talk to her like that. Then she slowly stood, her legs shaking so bad they could barely keep her up, and silently followed Maria and Kevin to the bridge. Vandergraf and Gary tried to follow them, Gary with the camera once again on his shoulder, but Kevin told them in no uncertain terms that recording was over. Maria was sure they would take that as more of a general suggestion than an order. For now, though, they at least relented. Gary even went up to the Gutsdorfs and asked them if there was anything he could do for the Japanese crewman, but Maria followed Kevin and Mercer to the bridge before she could see if Vandergraf followed his example and acted like a halfway decent person. Simon directed them while Cindy followed everyone else to the bridge.

Given the excitement and chaos of the last half hour the silence currently hanging over the bridge felt eerie, a reminder that something beyond their normal experience was out there and following some natural animal agenda they didn't yet understand. They let Mercer sit on a stool near the helm, but that was the only comfort they afforded her. It was still probably more than she deserved.

"Okay, time to talk," Maria said to her.

"Talk about what?" Mercer said sheepishly, quietly, almost as though she wasn't sure at all what trouble she could possibly be in. Maria remembered the way she had been acting that morning and compared it to the coldly calculating way her and Murphy had blown up a ship full of people. The time to believe her dumb and innocent act was over.

"Is Diane Mercer even your real name?" Maria asked.

"Of course it is," Mercer said. "Why would I have given you a different name?"

"If Mercer is your real name then you're an idiot," Maria said. "Because you can be damned sure that we would have reported your name to the authorities, and you even said it on camera where it was supposed to air throughout all of the U.S. But I don't think you're an idiot. Well, I still do, but not that big of an idiot. So let's try again. What's your name?"

For a second, Mercer looked like she was going to continue with the confused blonde act. Then it slipped away. Her eyes went cold and her mouth tightened into a grim line. "I'm not telling you my real name."

"Well, at least we've got that much out of you," Maria said. "So fine, we don't really even need your real name right now. When you're arrested, the cops will eventually figure it out for themselves. How about this then: who were you working with? Other than shark food out there?"

Mercer's grim look temporarily turned to one of horror, and out of the corner of her eye Maria thought she could even see Kevin grimace. The last thing Maria wanted to be was flippant about the death of another human being, but she needed to get past Mercer's defenses. And no matter how much of everything else they had done was an act, Maria was still sure that Mercer and Murphy had really been lovers.

"Are you sure he's not still out there?" Mercer asked. "Maybe he got away at the last second. If you send another boat out—"

"Maybe you missed it while you were being flung in the air, but I saw it very clearly. Murphy's dead." She paused, judging whether her next words were sincere, and decided they were. "I'm sorry."

"Oh God," Mercer said, putting her face in her hands and suppressing a sob. "This wasn't the way this was supposed to go. None of this. We were told it would be different."

Kevin and Maria both exchanged a glance. She supposed it was possible she was still acting, but the girl seemed legitimately torn up and confused. Maria nodded, indicating to Kevin that it was time for him to take over with a good cop side to their act. "Who, Diane?" Kevin asked. "Who was giving you orders?"

"Uh, I'm not sure if it was really anyone giving orders," Mercer said. "More like they were giving us a strong suggestion. And then making sure we had everything we needed. They said the bomb wouldn't be powerful enough to hurt anyone. It was just supposed to send a message."

"But who, Diane?"

"One Planet, of course."

Maria frowned. "No one in One Planet would ever condone this kind of action. No one. One Planet was specifically formed to be an alternative to environmental groups that were getting a little too drastic in their techniques."

"Well, that's who the guy said he was with. He said he was a representative of what One Planet really meant."

"No, Mercer," Maria said. "No one on this ship or with the One Planet organization would ever condone terrorism as a means to an end."

"Whoever he was, he sounded convincing enough to us. We both wanted to do something more than just stand in the way as another asshole raped the planet. This guy gave us the instructions on how to make the bomb and what to do with it."

"Did he ever give you a name?" Kevin asked.

"No. He said it would be better that way. He was wearing a suit when he came to us, though. An expensive one."

"And that wasn't your first clue that something was out of the ordinary?" Maria asked. "I've never in my life met a One Planet volunteer who would be caught dead in a suit. They tend to prefer Birkenstocks and tie-dyed shirts."

Mercer looked at her as though this was the first time this had occurred to her. "I suppose."

"Any other details you can give us?" Kevin asked. "The more cooperative you are at getting us out of this mess, the more likely that the authorities will give you some leeway."

"You think so?" Mercer asked. Maria didn't think so at all, but Mercer wasn't the only one who could lie.

"Yeah, I do," Maria said. "Any other details at all."

"Um, he had short brown hair. Very skinny. Fat chin. Oh, and I thought I saw a tattoo on his arm."

"What kind of tattoo?" Kevin asked.

"I couldn't really tell. It was mostly covered up by the sleeve of his suit, but a little bit of it was poking out near his wrist. Looked like it possibly could have been tribal."

Maria didn't think any of that was going to be useful, but Mercer should still have had one more piece of information they needed. "What were you supposed to do after the bomb went off?"

"There was a rendezvous point. Dave, uh, I mean Kirk had a GPS and we were supposed to meet them at specific coordinates not too far from here."

She gave them the coordinates and Kevin checked them against their current position. Unfortunately whoever was supposed to come pick them up would be just out of visual range for them.

"Was there any other way you were able to communicate with them?" Maria asked. "A specific radio channel or something?"

"No, we weren't supposed to have any extra contact with them. Once we met with them, they were supposed to take us back to the U.S. and make sure we wouldn't get into any trouble."

"And you believed them?" Kevin asked.

"Of course we did. Why wouldn't we?"

Maria knew that Kevin was more than smart enough to come to the same conclusion she did. Murphy and Mercer hadn't been anything more than patsies. They probably would have never showed back up in the United States. And One Planet would have taken all the blame for the attack, being labeled as ecoterrorists one and all of them.

And Maria's hope that they could use Mercer's escape plan for their own rescue was futile. They weren't going to get any help from that avenue. Instead, they were stranded here until the Mexican Navy arrived.

11

After much debate, they decided it wouldn't do any good to lock Mercer up somewhere on the ship. Any damage she could do was already done, and there was nowhere she could escape to. They were now her only hope to survive, and they made sure to emphasize that when they directed her to help the others with whatever they might need. Once Cindy escorted Mercer away that left Maria and Kevin alone on the bridge to try to make scientific sense of everything they had seen today.

"I'm not even sure where we should begin," Maria said.

"Let's just start by figuring out what questions we even need answered, starting from the beginning," Kevin said. "First one, how did all the hammerheads suddenly reappear at El Bajo when they should be all but gone?"

"Second question," Maria said. "Why are they so aggressive? Hammerheads don't usually see people as food. They might attack if they feel threatened, but most of what we were doing today had nothing to do with them."

"Right. And then there's the third question, literally the biggest and scariest one of all. Where did Teddy Bear come from and what does he or she have to do with everything else?"

"Oh dear God, Kevin. Please tell me you're not calling it Teddy Bear as well."

"It's as good a name as any other."

"No, it's really not."

"Look, that's not important."

Maria sighed. "I guess it's not. Here's another question, and I have to wonder if it's the most important one of all. Are the answers to all three of the previous questions the same?"

"We can't make that assumption," Kevin said, but he paused before continuing. "Yet it does seem likely. There's too many strange things at once for them to be unrelated."

"Did you get a good look at, uh, Teddy Bear at any point? Or the behavior of the other sharks?"

"No, can't say I did. I was a bit too busy trying to deal with the other crisis."

"Well I did. And I've got a hypothesis. It's crazy, but it's the only thing I can think of so far that matches the facts."

"And that is?"

"We could always try to say that Teddy Bear is just one freakishly large hammerhead of some unknown sub-species that just so happened to come along for the ride when all the other sharks decided to come back, but I don't think that's the case. I think Teddy Bear is the one that's causing this."

"You think she's, what, the leader of the other hammerheads? Don't you think that's a little far-fetched?"

"No, I think it's *very* far-fetched. Almost but not quite as far-fetched as a giant, previously undetected version of an endangered species."

"Okay, I'll take that point. But what proof do you have for your hypothesis?"

"The first is the fact that all the other hammerheads seem to go into a frenzy that only stops when Teddy Bear itself does something. The timing can't be a coincidence."

"Okay, there's that. What else?"

"The hammerheads are more organized than they have any right to be. You've taught me practically everything you know about sharks by now. And as far as cetaceous creatures go sharks are fairly smart, but they shouldn't be smart enough to coordinate attacks like that. Nothing we've been able to observe so far about any of the other sharks is out of the ordinary. Teddy Bear is the only x-factor."

"That we know of. There could always still be something below the surface here that we haven't seen yet."

"Okay, I'll give you that. There's one other thing, though. Teddy's Bears attacks so far haven't followed the same patterns as those of the other sharks."

"There's only been two that we've seen. That's hardly a reliable data sample."

"True, but those two have both been remarkably similar. Think about it. When did Teddy Bear attack the first time?"

"When Murphy and Mercer were just about to get away."

"And the second time?"

Kevin looked like he was starting to be convinced. "When you and the others got close to the point where Murphy and Mercer were."

"It seems to me that Teddy Bear is corralling us. It doesn't necessarily need to be the one doing that. It may be big and fast, but it would be more efficient if other sharks were keeping us from escaping."

"Okay, now you're starting to get unrealistic again," Kevin said. "You're attributing motives to it that it can't realistically have."

"How do we know what motives it can and can't have? We've never seen anything like it before. We don't actually have any real idea of what it's capable of."

Kevin stood staring out the window and thought about that for a minute. "So let's say for a moment that we go with everything you're saying," he finally said. "What would that mean if we put it all together?"

"I think it means that Teddy Bear is somehow controlling all the other sharks. It may be smart enough to have specific reasons and maybe even a plan. And keeping us from leaving is part of that plan."

"You do realize that is the kind of leap in logic that wouldn't stand up to scrutiny in any scientific journal, right?"

"Well, I'm not the scientist here, technically. Not yet. That would be you. Do your science. Poke holes in my theory."

Kevin nodded but said nothing. He went back to staring out the window where a few dorsal fins had resurfaced and appeared to once more be circling the *Cameron*. Maria waited for nearly a minute for him to reply, but he had gone off into his own little world. She'd seen him in this state before. He was taking all the data and examining it from every angle. He would stay that way for some time unless she interrupted his train of thought. For now, she thought that would be a mistake. Instead, she left him alone and went back out on the deck.

The somber mood of before had given way to one of restlessness. Maria could hear it in the quiet but angry murmurs of the Japanese crew as she stepped out into the sun. As she walked past them, several of the men gave her the stink eye, and one or two even looked outright hostile.

"Do I want to know what's going on?" Maria asked Cindy, keeping her voice low in case any of the castaways could understand her.

"My understanding of Japanese is spotty," Cindy said, "but Simon thinks he's watched enough anime that he thinks he understands the gist of it. They're angry."

"Well, yes. That part I was able to figure out without knowing any Japanese myself. And they have the right to be."

"But Simon thinks they're angry at us. No one has explained to them yet what happened."

"That's because we're only sort of starting to understand it ourselves."

"They do know that we're the ones who usually keep them from fishing in these waters, though, so it makes sense that they would blame us. And I think a few of them have finally recognized Mercer as the one who put the bomb on their hull. No one has explained to them yet that she's not really with us."

"Christ," Maria muttered. She was going to have to go back to the bridge and get Kevin to come out here and give them some kind of explanation, or at least one that would keep them from doing anything rash until they could all get rescued. She was just about to go back when one of the men shouted and began pointing out over the sea. Maria didn't need to speak his language to understand what had suddenly gotten him so excited. There was a speck on the horizon that was getting bigger. Even without the binoculars, Maria knew that it had to be a ship.

"Oh thank God," Boleau said as she joined the two of them. "About time the Navy arrived."

Except something about the ship seemed wrong to Maria. After some rummaging around for their equipment – it had been scattered as everyone moved everything around looking for additional first aid supplies – Maria found the binoculars again and focused on the speck. It was definitely a marine vessel, but she didn't think it was quite the right shape to be the Mexican Navy. She also didn't think that the Navy would have sent just a single ship, given that the sinking of a Japanese vessel now made this whole thing an international incident they had to take seriously.

"Huh," Maria said. "Well I'll be damned."

"What?" Cindy asked.

"I don't think that's our rescue."

"Then what is it?"

"I think it's *Mercer*'s rescue."

12

While the Japanese crew, and even Vandergraf and Gary, stood up and started waving their arms in an attempt to get the attention of a ship that was obviously still too far away for it to see them, Maria got Mercer and had her look through the binoculars at the approaching ship.

"Well?" Maria asked. "Is that it?"

Mercer put the binoculars down and bit her lip. "I don't know."

"You don't know what the ship that was supposed to pick you up even looked like?"

"No. They just told us someone would come for us shortly after they confirmed that we'd done our job. I didn't even know how they were supposed to confirm it."

"That didn't bother you in the slightest?" Maria asked. "Not a single red flag?"

"No! Okay, I'm starting to realize just how stupid we really were, but we trusted what they were saying. The guy had all the right words to reassure us. We just thought the lack of extra information was in case we got caught, so we couldn't give anyone away. Which I guess is working."

Maria cussed quietly to herself. While everyone else was convinced that help was on the way, she herself was doubtful. Nothing about the man Mercer had described made her think they were dealing with the kind of people that would save a bunch of people out of the goodness of their hearts. If anything, she was beginning to think they needed to keep that ship away at all costs. She said as much to Cindy and Mercer.

"But why?" Cindy asked. "In case you haven't noticed, we're kind of sort of in deep shit here."

"And I think we're going to be in it even worse if that ship reaches us," Maria said. She turned to Mercer. "You don't really think they were going to let you live, do you?"

"What? Of course they were. There was a plan."

"Diane, whoever the hell in on that boat has nothing to do with

One Planet. They were willing to frame the group and kill a whole lot of people in the process. They wouldn't have let some naïve young blonde get away when she had any kind of information that could link them to what happened today. Anyone who knew too much was going to go into the ocean and not come back out."

"Are you sure you're not just being paranoid?" Cindy asked. Her tone of voice was distinctly worried, however.

"Given the events of the last hour or so, I'd say staying paranoid is the healthy option for the moment," Maria said.

"So you're saying you're actually hoping these people *don't* come to help us?" Cindy asked.

"Given the fact that we're dead in the water and unable to get away from them, it doesn't really matter what I'm hoping. They seem to be heading this direction one way or the other. My only suggestion is that we be prepared for their intentions to be less than altruistic."

"Maria, sometimes I have to wonder about you," Cindy said. Yet at the same time she found a bag of emergency supplies nearby and grabbed the flare gun from it. For a moment Maria thought she would waste it by signaling the oncoming ship. Instead she just kept it in her hand like it was a more conventional gun. Maria herself grabbed the nearest prod and wished they had somehow been able to rescue Mercer's pistol before it had gone in the drink.

The closer the boat got the better Maria could get an idea of its size. It was significantly smaller than the *Tetsuo Maru* but still larger than the *Cameron*, about the size of a typical Coast Guard vessel. It didn't have any markings of the Coast Guard, however. In fact, Maria was hard pressed to find any markings on it at all, not even the boat's name or number painted on the side. If that wasn't an ominous detail, she didn't know what was.

"Can you see any of the people on board?" Cindy asked. Maria looked through the binoculars again and shook her head.

"Nobody. No one on the deck and it looks like all the windows are tinted."

"Seriously?" Maria handed her the binoculars so she could see for herself. "Aw shit. Mercer, what in God's good name have you gotten all of us into?"

Mercer didn't respond. Maria was happy about that, as she couldn't imagine anything coming out of the girl's mouth that could possibly be useful.

"Cindy, go around to anyone who'll listen and see what they can do about arming themselves," Maria said. She didn't add that she didn't think any preparations they made would make a difference. The more she looked at the oncoming boat the more she believed that Murphy and Mercer would have never been pulled out of the sea. And now that they hadn't found the couple where they were supposed to be, the boat was coming to make sure no one could point a finger at anyone for this disaster besides One Planet and their little group on the *Cameron*.

Kevin came out and joined them on the crowded deck. The Japanese crew was celebrating their impending rescue even as Cindy whispered in Simon's ear, who in turn went to find Monica.

"What's going on?" Kevin asked, and Maria filled him in on her theory with as few words as possible. Although it startled Kevin, he looked much more concerned about what was going on in the water. He pointed, and Maria realized she'd been so focused on the boat that she'd stopped giving any mind to the sharks. Although they stayed far enough under water that their fins didn't break the surface, she could still see that they were agitated again, swimming close enough to the surface that their forms could clearly be seen in the hundreds.

"Everyone get away from the sides," Maria yelled. Only a few of the Japanese crewmen heard her over their own celebrating, and those few that did, didn't seem to understand what she was saying. She had to physically pull several of them away and indicate the shapes in the water before any of them realized they weren't as safe as they had hoped. After half a minute, they'd gotten most of the people crowded together on the center of the already too small deck. If they got out of this alive she needed to see if Kevin would be amenable to getting a bigger trimaran.

All of the Cameron's crew and several of the Japanese men had found something to arm themselves with, ranging from one or two flare guns on down to oars, but the few armed crewmen from the *Tetsuo Maru* still didn't seem to understand why they needed them. Several of them waved their makeshift weapons at the water, which Maria supposed was a smart enough move on its own yet not quite what she was really worried about.

"So now what?" Vandergraf asked. He himself had found one of the prods that had been in the Gutsdorfs' Zodiac. It was a better weapon than the oars, yet if Maria's theory was correct and whoever was in that boat would be trying to kill them, she suspected it would be with guns. Prods wouldn't do much to stop a bullet.

"I… I don't really know," Maria said. She'd spent enough time on the water that she knew how to handle all kinds of emergencies, but the approach of a ship full of people who may or may not want to kill them was new to her. The boat was close enough now that she no longer needed binoculars to see the suspicious lack of a name or any identifying markings. "Mercer, please. If there's anything else you can tell us about these people, anything at all…"

"I don't know!" Mercer said. "I wasn't ever thinking that they might try to come kill me."

Maria looked down at the water again. The water was growing choppier with the volume of movement below the surface, although she noticed that there was nothing immediately surrounding the approaching boat. The hammerheads looked like they were avoiding it, but Maria had no idea why they would. They certainly hadn't tried to avoid the Cameron up until now or the Zodiacs. It was almost as if they were…

Wait, could that really be it? It seemed impossible, yet Maria had already seen three or four things today that she would have thought impossible at breakfast, so it no longer felt like such a leap in logic.

"This is going to sound crazy, but I think all we need to do is buy some time," Maria whispered to Kevin.

"Why?" he asked. "What do you have planned?"

"I don't have anything planned. However, I think the sharks do."

"Maria, that's crazy. They can't make complex plans."

"They also can't grow to the size of a small house or spontaneously reappear in a place where they were starting to look like they were extinct."

"That's true enough, but it's a logic leap nonetheless."

"Maybe it is, but it's the only thing we have right now. Unless you've got a better plan to get us out of this alive?"

Kevin sighed. "I can't say that I do."

"Then play along with me. Trust me, I know this is going to seem horrible, but I know what I'm doing."

"You're sure?"

"No, not even slightly. Quick, go grab the bullhorn before that boat gets within shooting range." She turned to Mercer and Vandergraf, neither of whom had been listening in on her conversation. Good. This would be easier to sell if Mercer thought it was real. "Vandergraf? Take Mercer so she's just inside the cabin, but keep a hold on her and be ready to bring her out when I say."

"Huh?" Vandergraf asked.

"Wait, what are you doing?" Mercer asked.

"Turning you over to them. You're the only one who really knows anything. Maybe if they have you they won't do anything to the rest of us." In truth Maria didn't believe that for a second. If the people on this boat had wanted the world to believe that rogue members of One Planet were really the ones responsible for the sinking of the *Tetsuo Maru*, then it wouldn't do any good for them to leave behind people that Mercer might have told the truth to.

"Wait, you can't do that!" Mercer said. "You're not serious, right? That's not the kind of person you are."

"Gary, can you get over here and give Vandergraf a hand?" Maria said. Gary came over with a clearly disturbed look on his face. He must have heard what they were saying.

"I'm not sure I'm comfortable with this," Gary said.

I'm not either, Maria thought as she directed the two of them to take Mercer by the arms. She didn't exactly feel much sympathy for Mercer right now, except she did feel wrong about telling two men she didn't entirely trust anyway to manhandle a woman. *If they do anything more to her than hold her steady I will neuter them both with my bare hands.*

They dragged her out of sight of the approaching ship just as Kevin came back with the bullhorn. It was standard equipment for these kind of trips where they might need to communicate with any offending ships in any manner of ways. Maria turned it on once she thought the ship was within hearing distance but maybe, she hoped, not quite close enough that anyone on board would easily be able to shoot them.

"This is a message for whoever's on that boat," she shouted. "We'd like to make a deal."

For several seconds, the boat continued to approach. Then it stopped rather abruptly. She still couldn't see any movement on the deck, and the windows to the bridge were tinted dark enough that she couldn't see inside. That was hardly standard.

"Maybe it would be better if we tried to communicate with them over the radio," Kevin whispered in her ear. Maria shook her head and turned the bullhorn off just long enough so the other ship wouldn't be able to hear her.

"No, I want to try getting someone out on the deck. We'll just pretend the radio is a busted as the engines." She turned the bullhorn back on. Now was the time to test her bullshit skills. "We have Diane Mercer, or whatever the hell her real name might be. We're willing to give her to you, but we want to talk terms first." She thought for a second and then added, "We have plenty of guns. If you try to get to close without our say so we will shoot."

"That's a bit ballsy," Kevin said in her ear. His voice had an interesting combination of worry, amusement, and perhaps a little bit of love. There was a reason he liked her, after all.

She lowered the bullhorn. "I want them to at least pause before they start shooting us."

"If that's really what they want to do," Kevin said. "We still don't know."

Maria shook her head. "At this point I truly doubt they're only here to bake us a cake."

Now they had no choice but to wait.

13

There were several minutes before anything else happened. The *Tetsuo Maru* crew was finally realizing that something was terribly wrong, and although Maria didn't understand what they were muttering, Kevin assured her it wasn't happy. Then there was movement on the deck as a gentleman came out and stood near the bow. He also had a bullhorn, although he fumbled with it for several seconds as though he had never used one before and wasn't sure how to turn it on. In her mind, Maria had almost expected a mysterious man in a black suit and mirrored sunglasses, but his appearance was much more mundane. He wore blue jeans, although they were a little too clean and crisp to be anything other than new. He also had on a plain red t-shirt with a pocket full of cigarettes over his heart. He did wear a life vest but it wasn't buckled. It didn't even look like he'd bothered adjusting the straps so it fit him, giving him the appearance that he was too big for his clothes even though he was rather short and skinny. This was not a man who was used to being on the open water, and he had trouble staying straight as the boat rocked beneath him. Maria noticed that the water underneath his boat was getting choppier by the minute even while the water around the *Cameron* calmed down.

Finally, the man got the bullhorn turned on. Even over the megaphone, his raspy voice somehow managed to sound soft-spoken. "Can I please speak to whoever's in charge?" he asked.

Maria paused long enough to look over at Kevin. He gave her an almost imperceptible nod. This might have been his boat and his mission, but in this he was giving her all his trust. She hoped she wasn't about to waste it.

"That would be me," she responded back through her own bullhorn.

Although there was just enough distance between them that it was hard for her to tell for sure, Maria thought the man looked surprised. That little flinch was a mistake. It told her that he knew she wasn't supposed to be the one in command. And if he knew that much, he probably knew exactly who was on this boat. A random ship floating through the middle of nowhere wouldn't have known that. Through that small movement he'd given up any chance of pretending he was not, in fact, here to pick up a fugitive saboteur.

She couldn't quite tell if he realized that, though, or if that had ever been his plan at all. He looked long and hard at the motley crew on the deck before responding. "You said you were armed. I don't see much in the way of guns."

"Just because you can't see them doesn't mean they're not there," she said. While she tried not to look away from the man, she was also trying to keep an eye on whatever might be happening in the water. Although she could see the tips of numerous dorsal fins now, there was nothing to exactly support her hypothesis that the sharks were actively planning something. Suddenly that entire line of thought seemed utterly ridiculous. She might just be gambling all their lives on a possibility that no self-respecting scientist would have ever entertained.

"I'm sure," the man said. She didn't even need to see him up close to hear the way his smug smile came through in his voice. "You said you have Diane Mercer. What about Kirk Murphy?"

Maria had almost forgot that they were supposed to pick up both of them. She saw an opportunity for a little more negotiating room. "He's not here, but we know where he is."

The man paused. Maria wished they were able to do this closer together. From this distance, she had some trouble reading his reactions. She supposed it worked in her favor, though. If she couldn't be sure about him then he couldn't be sure about her either. "Can you show her to me?" he asked.

Maria stopped to think about it just long enough to look at his ship and make sure there were no obvious places where a sniper or something might be. She gestured to Gary and Vandergraf standing just out of sight and had them bring out Mercer for just a moment. Once she was sure the man had seen her she waved them away. Mercer struggled against them as they pulled her back out of sight. She really was a dumb one, Maria realized. The last place she wanted to be right now was in the open.

"I do have to say, ma'am…" He thought for a moment then

shrugged. "I mean, Miss Quintero. I have to say that this is not how I expected this to go today."

Oh you have no idea, Maria thought. She risked a glance at the water and saw a large number of dorsal fins openly circling the man's boat. She still wasn't one hundred percent certain what that meant, but she hoped it was a good sign.

"I'm sure it wasn't," Maria said. "You seem to have me at a disadvantage. You know my name. Can I have something to call you?"

"Smith, I suppose."

"Seriously?"

"What did you expect, my real name?"

"No, I guess not."

"Smith is all you're going to need. Especially since I'm sure both of us want this to be over and done with as soon as possible."

She wondered for a moment if maybe she'd been too paranoid in thinking that he planned to kill them. Maybe it really was possible that they could get out of this just by turning Mercer over, that this man would take her somewhere far away where she would take on a new name that wasn't associated with a terrorist act.

There was movement near the bridge of the nameless ship. She wished she had the binoculars with her, because it had almost looked like the glint of sunlight on glass. It could be someone looking at them through their own binoculars. Or it could have been a sniper scope.

She looked once more down at the water. All at once the sharks dove down below the surface. The man was too intent on her to notice any of this. *Is that a good thing or a bad thing?* she thought.

"All we want is to get out of here alive," Maria said. "Is that something you think can happen?"

She thought there might have been a pause in his voice before responding. "Of course. Why wouldn't it be?"

There was another glint from somewhere behind him. She was sure it hadn't been her imagination. As she tried to follow it, she thought she saw what might be the barrel of a rifle poking out ever so slightly over the top of the bridge. It wasn't in the same place she'd thought she'd seen one earlier. There were at least two people on that boat with guns pointed straight at them.

She looked over to Vandergraf where he stood behind a wall just out of Smith's sight. He looked like he was about to take that as a sign to pull out Mercer again, but that was the absolute last thing any of them wanted right now. Mercer was the only one this man one hundred percent definitely wanted out of the way. If either of those snipers took her out then they lost all chance of getting out of this. She shook her head, hoping Vandergraf understood what that meant, and brought her attention back to Smith.

None of them ever got a chance to find out how far this stand-off might have gone, because that was when Teddy Bear made her presence known again.

Smith's boat suddenly rocked violently for no visible reason. Smith, already unsteady standing out on the sea as it was, stumbled and dropped his bullhorn over the side. It splashed in the water where a sudden violent white storm of churning water erupted around it before subsiding. Apparently the hammerheads hiding below hadn't found it very appetizing.

Everyone on the *Cameron* became agitated as Smith's boat rocked again. Kevin saw where this might head and took the initiative. He yelled something in Japanese, then repeated it English. "Everyone that can fit, get below deck!"

Maria didn't think there was enough room for everyone to fit inside, considering there wasn't even technically enough room for them to be on deck, but that didn't stop everyone from making a mad dash into the cabin. Maria and Kevin both jostled to stay in place, along with Cindy. She still had the flare gun in her hand. That was good, Maria thought. They might need it in just a moment.

Smith, for his part, didn't seem to have the slightest clue what was going on. He just knew that the ship shouldn't have been violently shimmying beneath him. He shot a comical look Maria's direction as though he thought she might somehow be responsible for this. Maria couldn't resist giving him a shrug in response, although any mirth she might have felt was short-lived. The boat rocked again, but this time it was accompanied by a violent splash large enough to soak her all the way back on the deck of the *Cameron*. It had happened too fast for her to be sure, but it had looked to her like Teddy Bear had come straight up from underneath to ram the boat. Even with the shark's abnormal size, she didn't think it could do any real damage, but it sure seemed determined to try.

Several other people suddenly appeared on the deck with Smith, one not making any attempt to hide that she was carrying a sniper rifle. The sniper didn't appear to have any interest in targeting anyone at the moment, though. Instead, she and the other man looked more concerned about getting Smith off the deck and out of any potential danger. Smith, still not appearing to realize how much danger he might be in, spent several seconds trying to keep their hands off him.

The movement got him just a little too close to the edge at the wrong time.

The boat was hit again, and this time there was no doubt that Teddy Bear was responsible. The giant hammerhead hit the boat with enough force that Maria could almost swear the entire front end came out of the water to show the shark's distinctly shaped head for just a second. The force was enough to send Smith and the man currently gripping his arm up off the deck. Smith went over the edge and the man looked for a split second like he might be able to land with the right stance to keep both of them from falling into the water, but Smith's weight proved too much for him and they both went over. The female sniper made no effort to help them, instead running back for the bridge as her apparent boss and coworker hit the water.

Smith didn't have the time to splash or flail about. Seconds after he went under, the blue sea around him turned red. The man who went in with him, however, wasn't lucky enough for it to be over that quickly. His head came back up after a few seconds, his hair slicked with blood and viscera that obviously didn't belong to him. He didn't appear to be aware of it, though, instead immediately trying to swim for the boat. But there was no way he was going to get back on board without a ladder or rope, and no one on board seemed too concerned about helping him. In fact, as soon as the sniper was back in the bridge the boat began to reverse, moving out of the man's grasping fingers right as he tried to touch the side. He cried out, more out of anger and surprise than any fear, but that didn't last long. The tone of his scream turned to something that was very clearly pain, then he dipped below the water for several seconds. When he came back up, the water around him was even darker red, although if it was coming from him he was in too much shock to realize it. Instead, he flailed until he was facing the *Cameron* and, probably realizing it was his only chance, started swimming toward it. He didn't get far before something below yanked him under again.

The water where he had been became calm again. Maria waited for him to reappear, only now realizing that she had her hands over her mouth to cover her shock and disgust. The man did come back to the surface, or at least a part of him did. An arm popped up, obviously not attached to anything, and bobbed there for a few seconds before a hammerhead snatched it and dragged it back below.

Maria would have thought that would be the end of it, but as the boat continued to back away as fast as it could, it continued to rock as though from its own personal earthquakes. The first couple were minor, as though Teddy Bear was unsure how to attack a moving target, but the third time Teddy Bear's shape came up from the side and caught some air first, slamming into the side and rocking the boat to a full forty-five degree angle.

"Oh dear God," Kevin said beside her, startling Maria. She hadn't even realized that he was still next to her. Everyone else had disappeared below, even Cindy by this point, but he stayed with her, his hand gripping hers tightly as though he were afraid she too could share the fate of Smith and the other man at any second. And, she realized, she probably could for as long as she remained on deck.

"We need to get inside," she said. Kevin just nodded in agreement.

14

Although the *Cameron* was not facing the right direction for them to see Smith's boat from the bridge, those who were crammed inside it rather than further below were silent enough they could all hear every thud as Teddy Bear relentlessly beat at it. Each sound got farther away as the boat tried to escape. Eventually the noises stopped. No one was sure if that was because it had gotten away or if it had finally taken so much damage that it had gone to join the *Tetsuo Maru*.

Somehow the silence that followed was even worse. Maria would have expected everyone to start talking or at least muttering to themselves to fill the quiet, but no one said anything. It was because they were expecting something else to fill that void for them, she realized. If the enormous monster patrolling the waters around them could practically sink a boat like the one Smith had come in on, then there was no reason it couldn't do the exact same thing to the *Cameron*.

Yet it didn't. For every second that passed by with them all still above the sea rather than below it, Maria became more and more convinced that her theories about Teddy Bear, no matter how ridiculous they seemed even in her own head, had to be right.

"Kevin," she finally said. Several of the men huddled near her startled at the sudden intrusion of her voice. "We need to talk."

"What, we can't do it here?" he asked. He practically said it directly into her ear. There were so many people in here that they were literally shoulder to shoulder.

"We could, but it might be difficult," she said. "Usually, in order to talk, people need to be able to breathe."

"I don't think that many people went below deck," Kevin said. Maria doubted that. She never had gotten a good head count on how many of the *Tetsuo Maru*'s crew they had rescued, but it was enough that more than a few would have had to escape to the meager quarters below. Still, she made her way through the shifting ocean of scared survivors and followed him down the steep stairs. To her surprise, it wasn't nearly as crowded down here as she had suspected. Which was to say she could still move, provided she didn't want to go more than a few inches at a time. Still, the ones who had ventured down the stairs seemed to be the younger members of the crew and as such were a little more adept at moving and shifting to let them through. They eventually made their way to one of the labs, which was where Maria had wanted to end up anyway. The aquariums and specimen containers that had been firmly secured to several of the shelves had still managed to get smashed or fall to the floor during the course of the day's misadventures, meaning that few people had wanted to walk through the glass-covered mess. One young Japanese sailor had worked his way to a semi-sitting position between the wall and a work bench, where he seemed to be much calmer than many of his fellow survivors. The other people who'd found their way in here were Monica Boleau and Simon Gutsdorf. Maria was fine with that. The fewer members of the *Cameron*'s actual crew that she needed to explain things to later, the better.

"So what is it, Maria?" Kevin asked.

"It's time we stop reacting to the situation and instead start taking an active role. We need to science this whole thing hardcore."

He raised an amused eyebrow. "I do think it's terribly sexy when you use science as a verb."

"Should we leave?" Boleau asked. "You guys are giving each other that look like you're ready to rip each other's clothes off."

"Which, you know, we don't blame you if the last thing you want to do before we all die is get your freak on," Simon said. "We just think it would be only decent if you didn't make the rest of us watch."

The young Japanese man said something, and despite the situation Kevin had to forcibly keep himself from laughing.

"What?" Maria asked. "What did he say?"

"Roughly translated? He said, well, maybe you don't want to know. Just realize that he can apparently understand English well enough, even if he's not speaking it."

Maria sighed. "For the love of Christ everybody, can we please get serious? Or would you all rather just jump one by one into the raging whirlpool of bizarrely violent sharks waiting just outside these walls?"

That forced everyone to quickly drop their mirth. "Okay," Kevin said. "Let's work the problem. What is it that you see?"

"It's not about what I can see," Maria said. She gently moved past Simon and Monica until she was at a metal chest near the far wall. There were a large number of components and scientific instruments in its many drawers, but the ones she was looking for were at the bottom. They hadn't expected to need these on this trip. In fact, for as long as the hammerheads had appeared permanently vanished from El Bajo, they had thought the money they spent on these things had been completely wasted. They were a part of the project that one of Kevin's colleagues had spearheaded a number of years ago, a hypothesis that had slowly gained traction in the marine biology community but had proved incredibly difficult to prove without any live hammerheads to use them on.

Finally, she found one of the things she was looking for. "It's not about what anyone can see, or any of the other four senses we all take for granted. It's about a sixth sense. Or seventh or eighth." She looked to Kevin and he shrugged.

"Honestly, with some marine animals who knows sometimes," he said.

Maria held what she had found up for everyone else in the room to look at. Everyone craned their necks to see, even the Japanese man. Admittedly what she held was so small some of them probably still couldn't see it in the room's unreliable light. When Mercer had destroyed the engines, she knocked out all but a few of the trimaran's emergency lights.

"That?" Kevin asked. "What does that have to do with..." He trailed off, getting what Maria liked to refer to as his "sciencing face." It meant he was working the problem in the same way she had, and probably with a lot more technical terms that she hadn't quite learned yet. Honestly, he probably would have come to the same conclusions she had if he'd been as up close to Teddy Bear as she had been instead of on the bridge.

"I don't get it," Simon said. He reached out to touch the thing in Maria's hand but she pulled it away. They had so few of them on the *Cameron* that they couldn't afford to lose this one, especially considering how many she thought they might need before the day was over. "What the hell even is it?"

The thing she had in her fingers, possibly their best hope at living through the day, didn't look like much more than a piece of translucent plastic not much bigger than her thumb. Inside were a number of electronic pieces that Maria herself couldn't quite explain. She was studying to be a marine biologist, after all, not an electrical engineer. Protruding from the plastic was a large, thick metal hook. If she handled it wrong, the hook could very easily rip through the tender pads of her fingers. It had better, considering it had been designed with the idea of breaking through that toughest of ocean hides, shark skin.

"A transmitter," Boleau said. Simon cocked his head at her and she shrugged. "What? This isn't my first rodeo. I've done plenty of volunteer work with One Planet. That included tagging beaked whales in the Pacific Northwest. Except this little puppy looks a little more heavy duty than the ones we used."

"That's because this isn't just a normal transmitter. The ones you've used were only to give off a weak signal that could be tracked to keep an eye on the whales' migrating habits. This, though. This has a very special purpose."

Kevin finally seemed to understand where she was going with all this. "Wait. Really? This is really what you're thinking?"

"Yes."

"It's crazy."

"Yep."

"It's ridiculous."

"Uh-huh."

Kevin stared down at the floor for several seconds before he looked back up at her, a distinct wild gleam in his eye saying that, despite the danger and horror of their situation, he was honestly excited.

"It may just save every single person on this boat."

15

"Alright," Simon said. "Could every person here stop being so cryptic and get on with explaining what the hell this little thing has to do with stopping a giant man-eating hammerhead? I feel like I'm in a bad movie on SyFy and that line you just said was the big cliffhanger before a commercial break. It's kind of obnoxious."

"You volunteered for this," Maria said, "but do you have a lot of training in marine biology?"

"Not really," he said. "Cindy's the fish buff. I've just been tagging along because it looks good on resumes. But I suspect this would be the part in the ridiculous killer shark movie where the two brilliant scientists explain the science of the situation in layman's term that even a drunk frat boy can understand after he got stood up for his Saturday night date and has nothing better to do than watch cable."

Boleau raised an eyebrow. "That was a little too specific for you to have made up on the spot."

"Bite your tongue," Simon said. "I would never join a frat. On purpose."

"Ahem, can I continue?" Maria asked.

"Oh, please do," Simon said. "We've only got about seven or eight minutes before the next commercial."

"So what I was trying to say is that there's been some speculation for a very long time that certain marine animals have a sense that humans do not. And not just marine animals, but also things like birds. You see, there has to be a way migratory animals can navigate enormous distances over the earth when going between their summer and winter homes. And the theory is that they can sense the magnetic fields of the Earth itself and follow it."

"Wait, you mean they can literally feel the Earth's energy?" Simon asked. "That's very hippy-dippy New Age."

"No, it's not like that at all," Kevin said, clearly annoyed that mysticism was invading his science.

"It's kind of like that," Maria amended. "But again, remember that I'm using tiny words for you and our viewers at home to understand. Could you please stop interrupting? If I'm right, we are sort of on a time limit before more people die."

Simon's smile went away. "Sorry. Go ahead."

"Right. So there's been a lot of study regarding this. It's all but been proven in geese. But it's a bit harder to tag and track and study things that spend almost their entire lives in an environment hostile to humans. There's been some studies with whales, if I remember correctly."

Kevin nodded. "And a while back several of my colleagues came down to El Bajo because they thought they'd found a way to one hundred percent prove it was also true with hammerhead sharks."

This part, at least, Simon seemed to understand. "But he couldn't do it, right? You can't study something that stubbornly refuses to be there."

"That's right," Kevin said. "If he had started his study ten, maybe even five years earlier, he would have found massive schools of hammerheads peacefully going about their business. He could have just tagged them with his specialized transmitters by taking a quick dive alongside them, and bam. Hypothesis proven. Instead, he spent his time wandering aimlessly searching the Sea of Cortez by day and getting drunk on my back deck by night."

"So now we have sharks," Simon said. "Yippee yay yahoo. If you ask me, this doesn't exactly seem like the best time to pull out old experiments."

"Probably not, but my friend's theories went a little deeper than just proving that hammerheads navigated using magnetic fields," Kevin said. He nodded at Maria. "That's what you've been getting at, right?"

"Yeah, it is," Maria said. "I know it seems crazy but everything we've seen so far seems to suggest it."

"Okay, being cryptic again," Boleau said.

"Sorry. You see, his hypothesis couldn't be proven just by tracking them. This…" She held up the little plastic device. "…can track them, but it also emits its own small magnetic field. The idea was that by manipulating the magnetic fields that the sharks felt, you could actually change their migratory patterns. If he put these on some hammerheads, activated them, and suddenly the sharks started swimming willy-nilly, then there he was. Theory proven and his name in all the scientific journals again. And if he could turn the devices on and off in the right patterns, give them fine enough control over magnetic pulses…"

Boleau perked up. "You could control the direction the sharks went. You could make them do whatever you wanted."

Maria shook her head. "Certainly a possibility, except the prototypes he made didn't have quite that level of precision. But yeah. In theory, someone with that kind of control could tell the hammerheads to swim left, swim right, go deeper or head to shallow water, just swim in circles, or do any number of things that might not usually make sense for them."

"Holy shit," Simon said. "Are you saying that everything going on outside is because someone is *telling* the hammerheads to go all Sharknado on us?"

"No," Kevin said. "Not someone. Some*thing*."

Maria watched as the truth dawned on both Simon and Monica. The two of them were too shocked at the idea to say anything. The young Japanese man, though, wasn't.

"Teddy Bear," he said in English that was much clearer than he had let on.

"That's right," Maria said. "He or she is the one factor that seems to be at the center of all of this."

"But it's not possible for a hammerhead to have the level of intelligence to pull this off," Boleau said.

"It's also not possible for a hammerhead to grow to that size," Kevin said. "And yet we can see the evidence otherwise just outside. It's entirely within the realm of possibility that whatever natural occurrence or mutation or modification, whichever the case may be, caused Teddy Bear to grow to that size also affected it's mental capacity. It's definitely not like sharks are stupid to begin with."

"You seriously think we have a genius level shark monster sitting out there?" Simon asked.

"Maybe not genius level," Maria said. "But with enough logical ability to have problem solving capabilities."

"But why?" the Japanese boy asked.

"Why is it doing this, you mean?" Maria asked.

"Yes."

She shrugged. "I couldn't tell you that one."

"Maybe you could," Kevin asked. "If you're still thinking about this problem in the same way I am."

Maria cocked her head. "Maybe I am. Care to tell me what you're thinking?"

"Wherever Teddy Bear specifically comes from, whether natural or man-made, there's enough true hammerhead shark in it that it came back here, most likely based on instinct. Maybe it did that in the past, maybe this is the first time. But its instincts say it needs to be here to mate and, well, it didn't find anything."

Simon gave him a blank look. "You're saying he's angry because he couldn't get laid."

"Or she," Maria said. "Either way, sure. She arrived, there weren't any of her kind here, so it calls others. Maybe she had to go around rounding them up from elsewhere, or maybe her magnetic manipulation ability is strong enough that she can call others over great distances. She fixes what she sees as a problem, but that wasn't enough. She really was pissed about the situation. She wanted revenge."

"Okay, now your theories are just getting ridiculous," Boleau said. "You two are supposed to be scientists or something. So don't make such huge leaps in logic. There's no evidence to suggest Teddy Bear has emotions and is being ruled by them."

"True enough," Kevin said. "But whatever the reason, there is still evidence that she has a plan. We've seen it."

"There is a very clear perimeter around El Bajo," Maria said. "The smaller hammerheads aren't going any farther than a certain distance. Also, there's what happened with Murphy and Mercer. Teddy Bear didn't show herself until they tried to leave that perimeter. And she showed herself again when the rescue Zodiac got too close to the edge. Now that we're here, it's clear that Teddy Bear doesn't want us to leave."

"And we still don't understand why," Boleau said.

"No, I think maybe we do," Kevin said. "Although I fully expect you to think we're crazy."

"I've sort of had that impression ever since I got on this boat,"

Simon said. "Might as well continue talking and keep the idea going."

"Okay, maybe we should be more careful than to assign any emotion to what Teddy Bear is doing," Maria said, "but the end result is the same. Whether she's angry and wants revenge for what was done to her breeding ground or if she's just really, really hungry, her end goal is the same. Don't you guys see it yet?"

"I see it," the Japanese man said. "We are, um, I cannot think of the word."

"Bait," Maria said.

"Yes, that is it," he said. "We are bait."

"Bait for what?" Simon asked.

"Other boats," Kevin said. "We come to El Bajo and we're not allowed to leave. Others come for us, like Smith and his mysterious people looking for Mercer, and they aren't allowed to leave either, but in a much more violent way. We continue sending out a distress signal for help…"

Boleau put her hands to her mouth. "And others fall into the trap."

Kevin nodded. "And right now we've got an entire Navy worth of people coming to help us and investigate the wreck of the *Tetsuo Maru*."

"Yeah, but so?" Simon asked. "These aren't going to be tiny rowboats they're sending. The Mexican Navy will be coming with huge ships, right?"

"And how big do you think a vessel would have to be to completely protect it from Teddy Bear?" Maria asked.

"I don't know. Maybe as big as…" Simon trailed off. He was finally coming to the same conclusion she'd come to earlier. Smith's boat should have been big enough to weather an attack. Although they couldn't be sure at this point whether it had sunk, they couldn't make the assumption that it hadn't, either.

"Someone should have kept an eye on our mystery ship," Boleau said quietly.

"Yes, someone should have. And then they probably would be food," the young man said.

"Nothing we can do about it now," Kevin said. "Instead we need to concentrate on what we *can* do."

"I still say we wait it out for the Navy to show up," Boleau said. "It's not like we can't communicate with them and warn them. You must have already told them what's happening, right?"

"None of the higher ups that I talked to seemed to believe me, at least not about the sharks," Kevin said. "Hell, they even sounded skeptical when I said we had nothing to do with the sinking of the *Tetsuo Maru*. I suspect we're going to need that footage Vandergraf and his man shot if we're going to avoid any kind of legal action."

"So maybe the fact that they didn't believe you doesn't matter," Simon said. "They're a fricking Navy. They can blast the shit out of anything coming at them."

Kevin visibly paled. "We can't just slaughter this creature."

"Kevin, honey, no offense but I don't think we can afford to take that kind of attitude right now," Maria said. "Teddy Bear is killing people. And if it's allowed to live, it will probably kill a lot more."

"Maria, what if Teddy Bear is an entirely new breed of hammerhead? Not just a single aberration, but the first specimen of a new species. There can't be many of them if we've never seen anything like this before. For all we know, we could be pushing a species to the brink of extinction on our first encounter with it."

"But we are in a situation where it could be kill or be killed. I understand your thoughts that we have a moral imperative to protect a possible new species, but if we talk morals then our true duty has to be to the people on this boat. Maybe it would be safer to let the Navy deal with Teddy Bear."

"Excuse me," the young man said, loud and clear enough that everyone else in the room immediately stopped and listened. "But do I and the rest of my crewmates not have some say in this?"

Maria took a deep breath. "Yes, of course. Although I don't think we really have the time to go around explaining the situation and polling every one of them."

"I was third-in-command on the *Tetsuo Maru*," the young man said. "Considering the first mate and my uncle the captain are gone, that gives me the right to speak for them."

Kevin cleared his throat. "I'm sorry. I didn't know you and Captain Ito were related. You have my condolences."

"He could be a son of a bitch, I believe is your term in English, but he was still family. So thank you." He turned to look at Maria. "Not everyone on the ship believed in what we were doing. I understand that the way my uncle fished for sharks was unsustainable. He saw money in it, but that money will be gone if there's nothing left to fish. If there is some way we can do this without destroying even more, I would put all my support behind it."

Maria nodded. A part of her had desperately wanted to wait for the Mexican Navy to show up and simply blow Teddy Bear out of the water. Another part had hoped someone would convince her otherwise.

But the problem was that more human lives would be put at risk with the plan she had in mind. No, she realized. Not lives plural. Only one person needed to do this. She already knew who it would be.

"Okay then," Maria said. "Then I know what needs to happen."

"What's that?" Boleau asked.

"I'm going to need to swim with the sharks."

The room went silent for several seconds, only to be interrupted by Simon.

"Aaaaaand… go to commercial break."

16

Maria gathered up all the specialized transmitters she could find while the inevitable argument ensued.

"Maria, you can't possibly be serious about doing this," Boleau said. Even in the cramped space of the lab, she had backed away as though Maria had caught a very special communicable version of crazy that she too might catch if she got too close.

"Someone's got to," Maria said.

"Then maybe Kevin is the one who should," Simon said. He looked at Kevin as though for support. "Right?"

Maria stopped what she was doing long enough to watch Kevin's reaction. Out of everyone on the boat, there were really only two people who could do this, her and him. She knew Kevin well enough that she already understood the shape of the argument to come, and he didn't disappoint.

"He's right," Kevin said. "Between the two of us, I'm the one who has the most diving experience."

"What about me? I have plenty of diving experience," Boleau said, although she seconds later she looked completely horrified as she realized what she was volunteering herself for. Lucky for her this wasn't only a matter of diving experience.

"This is going to need to be precision work," Maria said. "You may know your way around a scuba tank, but you've never tagged a live shark before. And even if you have, it probably wouldn't have been one that was actively trying to eat you."

"And you have?" Boleau asked.

"Sort of," Maria said. During one of her first times out with Kevin, they had been tagging some tiger sharks, most of them small. Kevin had warned her just in time as a much larger and more aggressive one had come at her from behind. It had scared her shitless yet she still, somehow, looked back at the memory fondly. She had been infatuated with marine biology before that, but the adrenaline rush of that instance had turned her feelings into outright love.

"Monica," Simon said, "maybe it's not the smartest thing for you to be arguing that you'd rather act as shark chum instead of someone else. I think something might be wrong with your survival instincts."

Once Maria had all the transmitters, she cast about the lab for the pole they used for tagging. It didn't look like there were any in here, so she gently yet firmly pushed past everyone else out into the hall. Predictably they all followed, even the young man who had been hiding away from everyone else.

"It should be me," Kevin said.

"We don't really have the time to make an argument of this, Kevin."

"I have a better chance if I'm the one the one to do this."

"Not really that much better. Have a little faith in your teaching skills. Besides, between the two of us, you're the one that's famous."

"That doesn't have anything to do with any of this!"

"Sure it does. Because when this is all over someone is going to need to talk about everything that happened here today. Between the sinking of the *Tetsuo Maru*, Murphy and Mercer's mysterious employers, and the fact that we've suddenly seen a brand new sea creature that shouldn't even exist, the plain and simple truth is that someone is going to need to inform the world, even it's just in the form of easily digestible sound bites on biased cable news networks. And let's face it, honey, yours is the face everyone would want to see, the only one they might listen to. And you can't do that if you're shark food."

"You're making it sound like whoever goes out there isn't going to come back."

Maria was about to say that wasn't true, but the reality of the situation finally hit her. She'd done plenty of dangerous things in the ocean before, yet this was the first time where she was honestly, truly scared for her life before she even started.

"That's because no one who has gone in the water when the hammerheads were in a frenzy has come back out," Maria said quietly.

"Mercer did," Simon said. They were all following her as she shouldered her way through the men crowding the hallway.

Farther down the hall Vandergraf stood, looking lost until he saw Maria. She looked away, hoping he wouldn't be able to get through to her before she found what she needed and headed back for the deck.

"And that's why maybe you shouldn't all be that worried," Maria said. She was aware that the words were more to convince herself than anyone else. "They're not just mindlessly savaging everyone. Teddy Bear is controlling them according to some kind of plan, whether or not any of us can agree what that plan is."

"My uncle might disagree, if he could," the young man said.

"Besides, I think we could use the transmitters to protect me while I'm in the water, so I'll need someone who can manipulate the signals properly from the boat. And you, honey, are better trained with these things than I am. If I were the one staying behind while you dove, it's much more likely that I would screw you up and get you killed."

Kevin made a pout that Maria would have thought cute under any other circumstances. "I'm not that much more trained." He seemed to understand how ridiculous he looked and regained his composure. "But I suppose you're right. I am the one who had to listen to him drone on about the engineering of these things while he was three sheets to the wind. Hopefully he didn't slur so much that I misunderstood something vital."

Maria made a face. "That's comforting." She grimaced even more when she saw that Vandergraf had found Gary again and they were coming toward her, Gary once again with the camera ready in his hand. Maria ducked into a nearby supply closet where she thought they kept the tagging poles, hoping that Vandergraf would lose her in the confusion of people outside. Unfortunately Kevin, Simon, Monica, and the young Japanese man still stood outside and gave her away.

She heard Vandergraf speak without turning around to look at him. "You have something planned."

"How could you possibly know that?" Simon asked.

"You don't get to be a reality television producer by missing the stories all around you. I'm trained to know these things."

Maria snorted as she found three poles buried behind some nets. "Sounds like an amazing skill. Don't know how the rest of us have survived this far without it."

She turned around hoping to see him look insulted, but her comment hadn't fazed him. "You all are planning something that can get us out of this, and I want to be around to see it."

"You mean you want your cameraman around to see it," Kevin corrected.

"They're the same thing."

"We don't have time for you to get in the way," Maria said.

"We're in the reality television business," Vandergraf said. "We know how to remain unobtrusive."

"If you're going to hang around then you're going to have to help," Maria said, shoving the poles into his hands. Vandergraf looked like he didn't know what to do with them. It was as though carrying anything for himself was a foreign concept. She turned back to Kevin. "Is this settled then?"

He came closer and gently held her arms. "I'll do my part. You just better be careful."

"Wait, isn't everyone here still forgetting something?" Simon asked. "Maria's not going to survive for five seconds once she jumps in the water, no matter what equipment she might have. The hammerheads are still going to swarm and shred her."

"No, I think we can prevent that," Kevin said. "As long as we're within a certain distance of the transmitters, we can still control what kind of signal they're putting out. They won't switch over to a preprogrammed signal until they're out of our range. So as long as Maria stays close, we can alter the magnetic frequencies from the transmitters she's carrying so they repel the hammerheads rather than control them."

"So they'll act as a shark repellent?" Simon asked.

"Up until a certain point, yes," Kevin said.

"Well, correct me if I'm wrong, but doesn't she, you know, need to actually get close to the sharks to do anything?"

"I'll just have to turn it off when she gets deep enough to attract Teddy Bear."

"And I won't be able to communicate with anyone on the *Cameron* once I'm in the water," Maria said.

"So let me see if I'm completely understanding what's about to happen," Boleau said. "Maria is about to jump into waters infested with an uncountable number of very angry hammerheads, looking for one big enough to sink a ship. She'll be unable to get anywhere near them, which she absolutely has to do, until Kevin, who won't be able to see or hear anything she's doing, flicks a switch. At that point they will probably swarm her and she'll need to find one specific one, stick it with a tiny transmitter, all the while trying not to get eaten. Do I have that correct?"

"No," Maria said.

"No?" Boleau repeated.

"No, I won't need to stick it with a transmitter. I'll need to stick it with two, one on each side of its head in order for us to be sure they'll work effectively."

"Oh, of course," Simon said. "Silly us. That's going to be sooooo much easier."

"Maria, this really sounds like a suicide mission," Boleau said. "You can't possibly think this is going to work."

"We might be able to figure out something safer if we had a shark cage on board," Kevin said. "But we didn't load it today because we didn't think we would need it."

"Look, there's nothing anyone is going to say that will stop me. I'm going to do this."

"And it's going to make for excellent television," Vandergraf said.

Kevin turned to Vandergraf. "Doug, I regret to inform you that we will not be doing any reality show with you. Sorry."

Despite all the terrible things that had happened today, Maria was tempted to say that the gobsmacked look on Vandergraf's face almost made it all worth it. Almost, but not quite.

17

With everyone capable doing their part to help, they estimated that they could have Maria ready to go in the water in less than fifteen minutes. That gave Maria and Kevin about ten minutes to be alone as Maria got ready.

"We can still wait," Kevin said. They were together in the small bedroom they shared when they took the Cameron out for longer periods of time. It was cramped, considering it had originally been intended as crew quarters while the original master bedroom had been converted into a lab. Despite the small space, they had spent some wonderfully intimate and sensuous times in this room, making love with the sounds of the waves buffeting the boat from outside. Maria got naked in front of Kevin now, but there was nothing sexual about it. She needed to change into her wetsuit and prepare for the chilly waters above El Bajo. Kevin likewise found nothing exciting about the moment, his eyes staying away from her bare skin and instead focusing on her face.

"No we can't," Maria said. "Not from a scientific perspective. You're the one with a doctorate here. I'd think you'd be all for risking my life in order to preserve a possible new species."

"You may love marine biology as much as I do, Maria, but sometimes I think you watch too many movies right along with Simon. I'm not a mad scientist here willing to sacrifice everything for a few results. You're more important to me than any shark will ever be."

Maria paused at that. There had been plenty of declarations of love between them by now, but this particular awkward admission felt like the most sincere she'd ever heard from him.

She also had to force herself not to smile because, despite his insistence that this was real life, his wording had sounded exactly like something written by a desperate screenwriter trying to shove a last moment of character development into the script before the final action sequence.

"I'm not going to die, Kevin," she said. "I have you watching my back."

"Except I can't actually watch it. You're going to be completely out of sight. I'll be able to use the transmitters to track the positions of you and any hammerhead you might tag, but that's an awfully limited field of vision. I'll be activating the transmitters based on guesswork."

"Speaking of which, shouldn't you be working on any final programming needed for the transmitters?"

"I told Gutierrez what we needed. He's better with electronics than I am."

"So it's not just you watching my back. It's him, and anyone else on the *Cameron* helping in every way they can. I'll be fine."

"For God's sakes, Maria. How are you able to be so calm about this? This is not a calm situation."

"Who said anything about calm? Kevin, I'm petrified right now," she said as she zipped up her suit and stretched to make sure the fit was right.

"You're not acting like it."

"What do you expect me to do, curl up and cry? I'll do that later when we're back at your house and snuggled up together in your bed. For now, I don't have the time or the energy for that. I need to remain focused. Probably more focused than I've ever had to be in my life."

"I just feel so helpless watching you get ready while all I have to do is watch. I feel like I'm doing nothing to contribute."

"Then don't do nothing. Do exactly what I need you to do."

"And what's that?"

Maria grabbed him tightly by the shoulders, her fingers looking pale as they pressed into his flesh. "Tell me I'm going to come back." She tried to say it smoothly and calmly, but her voice had an unexpected hitch.

Kevin held her shoulders right back. "You're going to come back."

They hugged each other tightly for several more minutes, not needing to say anything. The warm touch of the other person said it all for both of them.

By the time they both made their way back on deck, word of what Maria was going to do had spread to the rest of the crew as well as the refugees of the *Tetsuo Maru*. The young man they'd talked to downstairs, who'd finally introduced himself as Kyo, had spent the last fifteen minutes going around to his crewmates and explaining what was going on. While a few were still too shell-shocked by their experiences to be much help, most of the other helped in whatever way they could, including checking the scuba gear and ensuring that the remaining Zodiac was still sea-worthy. Boleau and Gutierrez had spent the time testing the transmitters and separating the ones that no longer appeared to work. To Maria's dismay that only left five for her to do her task. The Gutsdorfs, despite a healthy amount of whining on Simon's part, agreed to pilot the Zodiac so that it was directly over El Bajo, giving Maria the best possible starting point. Gary did nothing but film the entire proceedings while Vandergraf gave an inane running commentary. At least they both managed to stay out of everyone else's way.

"You have the equipment ready for the transmitters?" Kevin asked Gutierrez.

"Boleau's bringing it out from the bridge so you'll have a better view of the Zodiac from the deck," he said. "Not that the view will make you any less blind to what's going on down there, but I figured maybe it would make things a little easier for you psychologically."

"Thank you," Kevin said. He nodded in Kyo's direction. "Could you get everyone who's not going to actively be doing something during this back below? Not only are we going to need to keep the distractions to a minimum, but the last thing we want is for anyone to go flying if Teddy Bear suddenly decides to ram the *Cameron* after all."

As Kyo cleared the deck, the Gutsdorfs gingerly climbed into the Zodiac along with Maria's scuba gear. Kevin gave her a small pouch with the transmitters in it that went around her waist.

"You'll need to keep calm as you're handling those," he said. "If you drop any, it will be pretty much impossible to get back."

"Right," Maria said. Despite her best efforts her voice was shaking even more now.

"Hey, you can do this," Kevin said. He grabbed her by the arms again, which immediately had a grounding effect on her.

"Right. I can."

"Since we can't see anything you're going to be doing, it will all be about timing." He pulled out a waterproof watch and showed it to her. "Start the stopwatch function immediately before you go into the water. I'll have the transmitters set to repel the hammerheads for the first five minutes. That should give you some time to scout around and get your bearings. Then I'll turn them off completely. From then until you surface again, there's not going to be anything protecting you, so that's your window to stick Teddy Bear with the transmitters. Remember, it has to be at least two, one on each side, or else none of this is going to work."

"Right. I remember."

"As soon as you tag Teddy Bear, you need to get to the surface. When I see you that will be my signal to trigger the transmitters. We don't know if the effect will be instantaneous or not. It might take a moment for the magnetic signals to mess with Teddy Bear's control, so there might not be any time to wait. Get out of the water ASAP. You shouldn't be going down deep enough that you'll have to worry about getting the bends when you come up, but we'll have med supplies ready back on the Cameron if you need them so don't let that be something to worry you."

"Got it."

"Okay then. Last chance. I can still do this instead. Or we still might be able to get away with not doing it at all."

Maria glanced out over the water looking for dorsal fins. She saw a few. There shouldn't have been any. The hammerheads should have been gone, and she was risking her life to keep them here. When put like that, this really did seem like a crazy scheme. If she hesitated any longer, she suspected that she would in fact give in to temptation and back out.

"No. I've got this."

"Alright. See you when you come back up." He kissed her, long and sweet and sensuous. The feel of it lingered with her long after he backed away and took his place at the transmitter equipment.

She got in the Zodiac with Simon and Cindy, not allowing herself to look back at the Cameron as they motored out over the center of El Bajo. Maria put on the rest of her scuba equipment and prepped her tagging pole, putting one of the transmitters at the end before making sure the remaining four were secured in her pouch. It was entirely likely that the amount of time it took just to put on a transmitter underwater was all it would take for one of the hammerheads to kill her. As she worked she couldn't help but feel like there was something strange about the situation, but she couldn't place her finger on it until they were about halfway out.

"You two aren't bickering," Maria said.

Simon looked away. Cindy shot him an angry look.

"What?" Maria asked. "What am I missing."

"Don't," Cindy said, although Maria couldn't be sure if that was directed at her or Simon. Simon looked up at Maria with the expression of a dog who had just chewed up the sofa cushions.

"No really, what?" Maria asked.

"It's just…" Simon started, but Cindy cut him off.

"Don't say it. Don't you dare say it. If you say it, little brother, I will give you noogies for the complete entirety of our likely short remaining lives."

"I'm lost here," Maria said.

"It's just that this is always the point that something goes wrong," Simon said. "We have a plan which we've discussed openly. We're now on our way to execute it and everything is relatively calm. It's all a recipe for something terrible to happen."

"And I was trying to tell him earlier," Cindy said, "that's all well and good, but in those stupid movies the one thing that always sets the bad things off is people talking about how this is where things would go wrong. Or not go wrong. Any sort of open acknowledge of the formula is a guaranteed way to set things off."

"But we're not in a movie," Maria said.

"No, but…" Simon started. Maria cut him off.

"This is real life, not fiction. This is not a movie showing on Saturday night on SyFy. You know how I can tell? Not nearly enough blonde bimbos."

"Uh, there's Mercer," Cindy said.

"And Monica's sort of blonde," Simon said.

"Whatever. I'm Hispanic and Kevin is trans. Between the two of us, we're not nearly white and cis-normative enough to make it to SyFy. If this were fiction it's more likely that we're some hack pulp fiction writer's attempt at diversity. He's going to self-publish this on Amazon and tweet a little about it before the rest of humanity promptly forgets about it. But that's not going to happen either. Do you know why? Because this is *not fiction*."

They were both quiet for several moments before Simon murmured. "You can't really know that."

"I'll prove it to you," Maria said. "If we were in some badly written movie or novel, the writer wouldn't be able to resist a shark jumping out of the water and eating one of us right... now."

Cindy looked around, trying to be casual about it as though she didn't really expect anything to happen. Simon actively cringed. After several seconds of quiet, they both visibly relaxed.

"See?" Maria asked. "Real. This is reality with actual lives involved. So would the two of you please just focus?"

Absolutely nothing else happened for as long as Maria was in the Zodiac.

18

It wasn't until Maria was ready to plunge into the water that it occurred to her that the fact that nothing was happening was extremely worrisome.

Occasionally they would see some dorsal fins at a distance but there was nothing like the water-churning frenzy that had accompanied previous trips in the Zodiac. Maria wasn't the only one disquieted by the calm. As she did a final check of her equipment, Simon and Cindy softly bickered to each other, Simon complaining that any writer doing this story must have gotten it into his head to subvert genre norms just to mess with them and Cindy getting annoyed that he assumed the writer had to be a male.

"She probably has to write under her initials to hide the fact that she's a woman writing in a predominantly male genre," Cindy said.

"That's a pretty big assumption," Simon said.

"No bigger than assuming that we're all completely fictional. Here, does this feel fictional to you?" She pinched him.

"Ow! Hey, what the hell, are you twelve?"

"Would both of you please stop it?" Maria asked. "You're giving me a headache, and I kind of doubt I'll be able to take a Tylenol down there."

"Sorry," Cindy said. "Old habits for us. We fight when things are no longer exactly in our control."

Maria looked in the direction of the *Cameron*. She thought she could see the glint of sunlight on binoculars as Kevin watched her. She gave them a thumbs up and then, not allowing herself any more time to think about it or second guess herself, dove over the side.

She stayed at the surface just long enough for the Gutsdorfs to hand her the tagging pole. Then she let herself sink. She hadn't gotten up this morning with the intention of doing a dive, but she never passed up the opportunity to go down below and, despite their horrifying and precarious situation, Maria allowed herself just a few seconds to revel in the thrill. The entire world around her was a rich deep blue that would never be matched by anything in the world above. The water, even though it was cold, surrounded her and gave her a deep sense of warmth, of caressing her entire body and sensuously flowing over her.

Then the memory of everything she had seen today came back to her, and along with it came the terror. She was in a hostile environment where humans had never been intended to go. She had heavy equipment strapped to her back that existed for the sole purpose of keeping her from dying by breathing the wrong thing. If she went far enough down, the weight of the water would be enough to crush her fragile body. Also, if she went down too far and came up too fast, nitrogen bubbles would form in her blood, crippling her in agony.

And all that was just the dangers of the ocean before she factored in the giant homicidal hammerhead whipping its brethren into a feeding frenzy.

Maria gave herself just a moment to feel all that fear before forcing it to pass through her. She would allow herself to feel the terror later, once she had emerged from the ocean alive and able to talk about it. For now, that horror would do nothing more than distract her at a critical moment. If she ever wanted to again feel dry land beneath her feet, she had to stay focused.

The first thing she had to do was get her bearings and assess the situation around her. She had five minutes (or now closer to four and a half, according to the watch on her wrist) before Kevin would switch off the magnetic pulses of the transmitters. Looking straight down, Maria could see the shadow of El Bajo Seamount, that geological formation that had so attracted the hammerheads for time beyond human imagining. She had been in these waters before and knew she could dive deep enough to reach the mount itself with minimal effort, probably even being able to come up without taking the time to depressurize if she needed to. According to Kevin, there had once been a time where, when looking down at the seamount, divers would have been able to see a beautiful and delicate dance as hammerheads swam all in one direction around the underwater mountain, hundreds of them moving in and out of the concentric circles in a show of mating prowess that was completely alien to human minds. Maria had never seen it. Those days when marine biologists had first discovered the wonders of El Bajo had been before she was even born, possibly even before her parents had met. Kevin himself would have only been a child. By the time Maria had joined up with Kevin and first seen El Bajo for herself, it had been nearly barren, schools of fish patrolling it now with no regards for the safety hazard this area had once provided for them. If she'd been lucky she could still see a small handful of small sharks, not large enough to cause a human to so much as slightly fret. Hammerheads by then had been a rarity, a special treat that was usually only glimpsed from afar. Like Bigfoot, they would be gone before she could be certain that it hadn't been an illusion.

What she saw now was no illusion, although it was far more unbelievable than any sasquatch sighting. Kevin had said that, at the height of breeding season, biologists would have been able to see hundreds of hammerheads at a time. However, just a rough guess based on what she was seeing now, there had to be nearly two thousand hammerheads circling clockwise around El Bajo. The sea below her was a roiling carpet of sharks, a school so thick she couldn't see the water beneath them. The circle spread out on either side of the seamount far enough that Maria couldn't quite see the edge. She stared down, the marine biologist in her taking over from that primal instinct to swim away as fast as she could. Maria tried to track the movements of individual sharks, knowing that the females tended to stay closer to the center and the males that could keep up with them were more likely to mate.

Close to the seamount, amid the boiling sea of sharks, a single dorsal fin briefly appeared that dwarfed all the others before disappearing once again.

This was why there were barely any sharks on the surface, Maria realized. In layman's terms, Teddy Bear was horny and wanted to get laid. And when one hammerhead that had the ability to control others wanted to get laid, they all wanted to get laid. She was witnessing a shark orgy of previously unknown proportions.

This was both a good thing and a bad thing for Maria. She checked her watch again. It had been about three minutes so far. When her time was up and Kevin disabled the protective magnetic field generated by the transmitters, many of the sharks would probably be too distracted to come for her. If they sensed her presence now, their desire to get rid of her would overwhelmed by their instinct to mate. But given Teddy Bear's tendencies so far, she wouldn't be surprised if any attempt to disrupt them was responded to with deadly hostility.

Not that she hadn't already been expecting that. The key here would be getting past all the other sharks to reach Teddy Bear. She decided to test the usefulness of the transmitters while they were still on, diving lower and angling farther out from the seamount. The closer she got, the more the hammerheads thinned out around her. She'd half expected a mad scramble to get away from her, as any mammals on the surface might in reaction to a sudden loud and screeching noise in their midst. That didn't appear to be the case here. It was more like the hammerheads interpreted her as a large boulder or some kind of land formation suddenly appearing among them that they effortlessly swam around. She moved back up away from them and again checked her watch. One minute. If she was going to come up with any kind of plan, she was running out of time to do it.

She again saw Teddy Bear's monstrous form appear briefly among its brethren, this time rising and then falling back below the others on the far side of the seamount. She mentally made a quick estimate of Teddy Bear's speed and the distance she had to swim around the seamount.

An idea came to her. A horrible, awful, brilliant idea. She didn't have any time to think about it. Her window of opportunity would be short, and she would need to swim quickly. Before she had an opportunity to convince herself this was nothing more than the quickest possible way to commit suicide, Maria dove once again for the mass of sharks below her, this time angling herself closer to the seamount.

She aimed right for where she calculated Teddy Bear's path would bring her when she came back around.

The sharks once again opened up in front of her. Instead of stopping before she went too deep in like earlier, Maria plunged deeper, going down until the wave of hammerheads crested over her invisible magnetic bubble. There were now sharks above her, sharks below her, and sharks on all sides. She looked at the watch again. Thirty seconds before her protective field vanished and she would be completely surrounded by very angry apex predators. She hefted the tagging pole in her hand, making sure she had a good feel for it. The last thing she wanted to do was misinterpret its weight and drop it at the worst possible moment.

Twenty seconds, the watch said.

Maria quickly checked the pouch hanging from her waist but didn't unsnap the clasp yet. She was probably going to need to move fast, and while she wanted the remaining transmitters to be handy right away she also didn't want them to go flying out into the ocean if she made sudden evasive maneuvers.

Fifteen seconds.

She tried to breathe normally. Using the rebreather was already counterintuitive, but it was even worse when her heart was pounding and her lungs desperately wanted take in more air than they could get. She wondered for just a moment if this was what it was like standing in front of a semi-truck as it roared down the freeway as she hoped the driver would see her in time and swerve.

Ten seconds.

Oh God, this is it, isn't it? she thought. *I'm going to die in…*

Nine seconds.

What if I got the timing wrong? What if…

Eight seconds.

I shouldn't have been the one who volunteered. Someone else could have done this, couldn't they?

Seven seconds.

Was this really even something that had to be done? I could have just waited for the Navy to show up…

Six seconds.

Oh God, oh God, oh shit, oh fuck, oh God…

Five seconds.

Okay, that's enough.

Four seconds.

Time to focus.

Three seconds.

I can do this.

Two seconds.

I can.
One second.
Oh shit.
Zero.

19

For several seconds nothing happened. The sharks continued on with their oblivious mating dance, moving around the bubble of magnetic force as though they were completely unaware than an intruder was in their midst. Maria almost wondered if something had gone wrong on the *Cameron* and she should get out now. Once her opportunity was gone it didn't seem likely that she was going to get it back, and she sure didn't want to be here among thousands of angry hammerheads at the wrong moment.

The protective bubble collapsed. She almost didn't realize it had happened. One second the sharks were steering completely clear of her, the next every one of them swimming around her started swimming in obvious agitation and confusion, no longer keeping their distance but not sure whether it was safe to get closer to her. Maria imagined it would be like leaning against a solid wall that suddenly vanished for no apparent reason and the sharks were now doing the under-sea equivalent of trying to regain their balance. The ones swimming directly toward her no longer tried to swim around, although most of them still kept their distance. One swam so close that she could have brushed its distinctively shaped head, like petting a confused stray cat.

Then Teddy Bear was in front of her.

She'd judged her timing and distances well. She was directly in Teddy Bear's path, and although she had expected the enormous hammerhead a few seconds earlier, she was still in that brief period of time where all the creatures swimming around her were more perplexed by her presence than angry. That wouldn't last long, but then again she didn't think she needed long.

She held up the tagging pole like she was about to throw a spear. All she needed was two transmitters, one on each side of Teddy Bear, preferably as close to the head as she could get. According to the theories of Kevin's friend, it would be the magnetic equivalent of putting reigns on a horse. Just one would be enough to thoroughly confuse Teddy Bear, but they couldn't be sure that her ability to control the other sharks would be disrupted. She might just be get angrier and order the other hammerheads to kill Maria that much faster.

Or their theories about Teddy Bear controlling the others with magnetic waves were completely off base altogether. In that case, all Maria was about to do was hit a very angry, very huge shark in the head and make it even angrier.

She didn't have the time to think about how that particular scenario might play out. Teddy Bear was now upon her, and as quickly as Maria could move in the water she thrust the pole at the left side of the shark's head. Ideally she would have taken the time to get a better angle, ensuring that the transmitter's hook completely penetrated the hammerhead's thick skin and wasn't going to pop off at an inappropriate time. The pole still hit its target, though, tagging Teddy Bear just over the eye.

Maria didn't have time to move out of the way. The shark hit her head on, literally, its battering-ram shaped head smashing into her hip and sending her tumbling sideways through the water. The water around her cushioned the blow somewhat, but not enough that she didn't feel the sudden searing pain race up her side. She had just enough presence of mind in the moment to check that she wasn't bleeding before trying to swim out of the way of all the other hammerheads no longer ignoring her. She didn't have a lot of time, she knew. Their confusion couldn't last much longer, and she needed to not be smack dab in the middle of them when they came to their senses. She swam up, doing her best to ignore the pain while also trying to unsnap her pouch to get another transmitter. She came up out of the wall of sharks easily enough, but two of them aggressively darted toward her even as she made her way out of the school. One missed her and then disappeared back below into the pack of its fellows. The other came at Maria's leg, its mouth open and clearly ready to bite the unwelcome invader. It was a smaller one, at least, and a quick wave of the pole smacked it across the snout. It dashed off, leaving Maria alone for the moment, but she knew that was not going to last more than a few seconds.

Looking back down, she saw that the circle of sharks was breaking up. Apparently her disruption had taken them out of the mood. Maria had a brief random memory of a time several years back when, while in bed with a sexual partner and right before she could orgasm, he had gotten a call on his cell and stopped everything just to answer. She'd been pissed. Now she imagined those same feelings being shared by well over a thousand sharks, each of them suddenly in search of the rude jerk who had cockblocked them.

She fumbled the pouch and looked down just in time to see one of the transmitters fall out of her reach, disappearing between the writhing shark bodies. Only three left. That was fine, but it gave her little room for error. She pulled out a transmitter but didn't have time to snap the pouch closed again before she saw Teddy Bear erupt from the hammerheads on the far side of the seamount. The sharks below her were also breaking formation, although even in the increasing amount of chaos they all managed to move together in a strangely delicate dance. Maria desperately swam to the surface, her survival instincts dictating her moves even though she knew that heading away from her targets would hardly help her mission.

As she moved, she put the transmitter on the end of the tagging pole and twisted to get a clear view of Teddy Bear. The monster swam away farther into the murky depths, far enough away that she almost lost the hammerhead's silhouette in the gloom. She could still see just enough of Teddy Bear's shape, however, to know that she was turning around and was about to head back in Maria's direction. And with a creature that size, it would take no time at all to cover the distance.

Come on, it's just like bull fighting, Maria said. *Which I've never done. And under water. And with something that can bite me in half in one chomp. Okay, so not like bull fighting at...*

There wasn't any pain at first, just pressure. Then an exploding agony ripping through her body starting from her leg. She flipped in the water before she could realize what had happened, but she saw swirls of red trailing around her and knew it had to be her own blood. A hammerhead swam up past her with what looked like a piece of her wet suit trailing from its mouth. In her moment of distraction, she'd forgetting to watch below her as well as in front of her. Now that her body was doing a slow uncontrolled spin, though, she saw that the hammerheads had taken a formation like a long, ever-shifting spear. The first shark had hit her dead on, taking a chunk of her calf with it based on the searing pain, but she could still feel it. Her leg was still there, or at least mostly.

There was no more time, no more chance. Her mission wasn't done, but she had to surface if she wanted to have even the slightest chance of surviving now. The ruined leg would make swimming harder, and she had attacks coming at her from at least two directions. She had to go. Now.

She didn't move.

A part of her mind screamed at her that she was crazy, that she had a death wish, that this was a sure fire way to make sure she never saw dry land again. But another part was talking to her in a strong, confident, and quiet inner voice.

Focus. Be aware. See everything around you but be distracted by nothing.

The pain went away. The hazy red swirls floating in front of her face went away. The hammerheads below her and coming up fast did not go away, yet she compartmentalized them in her mind. They were something to worry about in a few seconds. Before they would reach her, however, there was Teddy Bear. The enormous creature was coming for her, clear to see, her mouth wide and aimed directly for Maria. The speed was uncanny.

Maria adjusted her arm slightly to compensate for her movement. Then, before she could give herself any more time to second guess her actions, Maria threw the pole exactly like a spear.

She missed the spot where the transmitter was supposed to go. Then again, she had intended to miss.

With her leg injured there was no way she would be able to out-swim the hammerheads coming up for below. She knew this. She was not a thing of the water. Real speed was not something she could accomplish here.

But Teddy Bear could.

The pole went low, perhaps a little lower than she'd intended. In those few microseconds, she'd had to come up with something she'd thought hitting her in the snout might be enough or, even better if she could somehow get the angle right on Teddy Bear's head, giving her enough of a jab in the eye that she would swerve.

Instead, the pole sliced through the water and jammed right into Teddy Bear's mouth, where it got caught in her lower teeth. It was enough. Teddy Bear veered slightly to her right and down, instinctively protecting herself from whatever bizarre attack her prey had suddenly thrown at her. The fin on Maria's left foot was clipped by Teddy Bear's head, again making her want to scream as she felt the fresh pain of what might just be a broken foot. Yet even through the increasing torment, Maria remained aware that, in this brief moment of time, Teddy Bear was between her and all the other hammerheads heading to rip her to pieces. And also in front of her, moving so quickly that she almost missed it, was Teddy Bear's dorsal fin.

Maria reached out and grabbed it, desperately holding on for dear life as the sudden acceleration nearly pulled her arms out of their sockets. Her grip held, just barely. She was now barreling through the water at the speed of giant mutant shark.

She quickly lost all sense of place as Teddy Bear raced through sea, desperately bucking and jerking in an effort to get her off. She could no longer tell where El Bajo was, nor where the Zodiac might be above her. As Teddy Bear flopped and thrashed and turned, she even lost all idea of which direction was up and which was down. She knew that might become a major problem when the time came to make her final mad swim for the surface, but for now she couldn't be bothered with that. The force of the water rushing against her threatened to tear her from her perch and send her falling back into whatever might be following, yet for now, miracle of miracles, she managed not to fall off.

Of course, it took both hands to hold on. She would have to let go long enough to grab one of her remaining transmitters, assuming they hadn't already vanished into the deep blue during her wild ride. She also felt the drag of the water on her rebreather, meaning if she didn't do this quickly she was just as likely to lose it and drown as she was to get eaten.

Pulling herself as close to Teddy Bear's body as she possibly could to reduce drag, Maria let go with her left hand and reached down to her pouch. By some happy cosmic accident, both transmitters had remained inside despite the open clasp. She had one in hand yet hesitated for a moment, something she knew she couldn't afford. The placement of the transmitter would make a difference. Hooking it anywhere into Teddy Bear's skin would theoretically cause the desired effect, but for best results she knew it should be up near the shark's head, preferably on the opposite side from where she was now. Unfortunately she didn't have the slightest idea how to accomplish this. Simply holding on was already proving to be too much of a test, let alone climbing onto the hammerhead's other side and crawling up to reach the ideal position.

Anywhere at all is going to have to do, she thought. *Just stick it in and pray it's enough.*

That was when Teddy Bear chose to make a particularly sharp turn. Maria's fingers tore loose from the fin and she found herself falling back from the monster.

But not before she reached out one last time and hooked the transmitter right into Teddy Bear's dorsal fin.

20

One enormous hammerhead swimming away from her on one side, thousands of enraged sharks on the other and below, everything below her ribcage pulsing in intense pain, and she wasn't completely sure which direction she needed to swim to get to the surface. Even as Maria allowed herself a moment of triumph, she realized it likely wouldn't last long. She would probably be dead within a few seconds.

That didn't mean she had to swim idly by and let it happen. If all she had was seconds then she was going to make them count. The first goal was to get some sense of orientation. She could swim for dear life all she wanted, but none of it would matter if, in her panic, she swam deeper into the ocean rather than toward the surface.

While the massive circle of sharks around the seamount had mostly broken up in the chaos, she could still see the largest portion of them in one particular direction. Using them and their orientation as her guide, Maria looked around until she could finally see the light of the sun filtering down from above. Okay, so she knew which direction she had to go. Now it was just a matter of getting there while she was missing a flipper on one leg and bleeding out from the other.

She wasn't sure exactly how much distance there was now between her and the surface, but she could see that Teddy Bear had brought her up closer. A quick glance down and around her showed several hammerheads circling and getting ready to go in for the kill. There was no way she could out-swim them. She did, however, have one last desperate idea that might buy her enough time.

Maria did her best to swim up as far as she could before the first hammerhead reached her. Even as she moved she undid the clasps on her scuba tank, getting ready to shed it. She took several deep breaths as she watched the first shark approach, then twisted around so the tank was between her and the shark. Maria shed the straps and pushed herself away from the tank, using it to give herself a little more momentum to get to the surface. If she'd timed it right then the hammerhead would get a tank right to the snout and, if she was lucky, temporarily get tangled in the straps. She didn't dare turn to make sure, though. From this point on, she couldn't look back. It was the surface of bust. Or get torn apart. Or drown. Whatever.

With her lungs full of a last bit of air, Maria did her best full stroke, kicking furiously with legs that didn't want to move and were probably leaving a trail of blood like breadcrumbs for the hammerheads to follow. She couldn't think about that. She couldn't think about how her chest suddenly burned with the need to breath. She couldn't even think if she was going to come up anywhere close to the Zodiac or if she would be so far away that the sharks would rip her into lunchmeat before Cindy and Simon could reach her. Instead, as darkness began to creep into the corners of her vision from a lack of air, Maria thought of the soft bed she had left behind at the house on the Baja Peninsula, of Kevin curled up next to her as his light snores vibrated the unruly hairs of his beard. She thought of days spent on the *Cameron*, watching whales breach so close nearby that she could reach out and occasionally touch their smooth, tough skin. She thought of her family back home in California, her mother and father and two younger brothers blissfully unaware that she might only have seconds more to live. She didn't want to lose any of it. And in that moment, any fear that might have been threatening to overpower her gave way to pure, unadulterated determination. She could be afraid later, back on the deck of the *Cameron*, as she realized what impossible feat she had just pulled off. But here in this moment it would do her no good.

She closed her eyes. Seeing how close she was or was not to safety wouldn't help. Maria just kept herself oriented up and pushed her body as hard as she could, her muscles burning at the effort, her entire being screaming for more air. Behind her eyelids she saw flashes of light, the signs that her air was giving out and, any moment now, her mouth would reflexively open to breathe and get nothing but lungs full of saltwater for its effort.

Oh God, I'm not going to make it. I'm not…

Her head broke above the water. Maria gave a great screaming gasp at the strangely delicious taste of fresh sea air.

"There! She's over there!"

In her adrenaline rush, she almost didn't recognize the voice as Simon's. In fact, it took her several moments to recognize the sounds as words at all. She was too busy relishing the fact that she was actually alive.

Of course, as long as she was in the water there was the possibility that she wouldn't be living for long. Maria looked around for the Zodiac and found it about five hundred feet to her left. She took a deep breath and started to swim in that direction, but it became obvious quickly that she had already used most of her inner reserves just reaching the surface. Thankfully the Gutsdorfs took the hint and piloted the Zodiac to meet her. Maria kept expecting one of the hammerheads to come up behind her and pull her back below at the last second. That was usually the way of it in Simon's movies, at least. But again, as she had repeatedly told him before, this wasn't fiction.

Simon reached over the side of the Zodiac and pulled Maria in. Now that she was out of the water the full extent of the damage she'd taken hit her, and every tiny movement as he pulled her all the way in was searing agony. She looked down at her right leg as it came out of the water, thinking at first that she must have been seeing some trick of the light. Cindy's choked back gasp of shock, however, told her that she wasn't hallucinating. She couldn't rightly be said to have a right calf anymore. There were certainly parts dangling from her ravaged leg that could still be identified as a calf if someone squinted, but that would require that person to look at the bloody mess to start with. Maria looked at it and didn't think much about it at first. She was more curious about the visible insides of her leg's anatomy than anything else.

Oh, I see. I guess this is what real shock feels like, she thought dispassionately.

"Oh God, we've got to get her back before she bleeds out," Cindy said.

"Wait... signal the *Cameron*," Maria said. She was surprised at the weakness of her own voice. "Tell Kevin... to activate the transmitters."

"We radioed him as soon as we saw you, just in case he didn't see himself."

"Oh. Good." Maria felt the overwhelming need to lie back in the soft bottom of the Zodiac and take a nap. It didn't have to be a long one. She was just so tired. As much as she tried to force herself to stay awake, she didn't think she could stay conscious much longer.

"Christ, she's fading," someone said. Maria thought it was Cindy, but she could no longer be sure. A noise jolted her to a higher level of wakefulness for just a few seconds. Her addled brain took abnormally long to recognize it as the Zodiac's motor as they rushed back to the *Cameron*.

"Did you do it?" someone else – Simon maybe? – asked.

"Do what?" Maria mumbled.

"Get the transmitters on Teddy Bear?"

"Oh. Sure." With hands that barely worked the way they were supposed to, since they were now cramping up from the death grip she'd had on Teddy Bear's fin, Maria reached down to her pouch and pulled out the last transmitter. "Even have one left."

"Oh shit, no," Simon said.

"What?" Cindy asked.

"Don't you see? She still has one left."

"So?"

"So that's not the way it works in those damned movies. There's always some dramatic thing where the hero has to accomplish the last task at the last moment. If she still has one then it means that this isn't over yet."

Maria roused herself just enough to make her indignation heard clearly in her voice. "For the last fucking time. This… is

not… fiction."

Teddy Bear hit the Zodiac from below.

Maria suddenly had to wonder if Simon was right. Maybe this was a movie. Because in a movie, that final dramatic moment often tended to be in slow motion so the audience could see the final time where the hero acted like a badass. And for the next several seconds time felt slower to Maria giving her one last brief period of complete lucidity before she lost consciousness.

The Zodiac rose up beneath them. Maria imagined that, to the people still on the *Cameron*, they looked exactly like Murphy and Mercer had earlier in the day right before Teddy Bear chomped Murphy into bloody bits. The angle that Teddy Bear came at them, though, must have been different because the raft spun as they all flew in the air, allowing Maria one last long look at the majestic and terrifying creature with an idiotic name. Teddy Bear was below them at an angle, trying to snap at Cindy as she fell but coming up far short. From here, though, Maria could clearly see the spot where the transmitter should have been on Teddy Bear's dorsal fin. It was gone. That probably explained why the hammerhead wasn't as precise in her strike as she had been earlier. The one transmitter was enough to mess with her navigation, but not enough to control her outright.

Even as she flew up in the air and began to tumble back down, Maria realized she still had the last transmitter in her hand. One last chance to save everyone.

Maria reached out as she fell, her hand brushing Teddy Bear's skin one last time, almost as though she were caressing a beloved pet. Despite her terror, she felt an instance of strange affection for the hammerhead, an appreciation for its savage beauty even as it made a final attempt to kill her.

The transmitter's hook went into Teddy Bear's skin, this time on her head exactly where it was supposed to be. Maria didn't have the time to feel any triumph, though. That was when time felt like it sped up again, and she hit the water before she realized what else was happening.

And everything went black.

21

Maria woke up two days later in a hospital with a cast on her left foot, various abrasions and braces on her arms, and more tubes going in and out of her body than she was capable of counting in her groggy state. It took her several additional minutes of trying to take in her surroundings before she realized that the shapes under her blankets stopped just below her right knee.

A couple minutes later, after a nurse came in and found her awake, they sent a doctor in to explain to her what she had already realized. In broken English (and then clear Spanish when she said she spoke it), the doctor explained that when she'd finally been brought in she was close to death, and the medics on the Navy ship that had rescued the *Cameron* had needed to use defibrillators to restart her heart at one point. In the midst of it all someone had determined that the only way to save her was to lose what remained of her right lower leg. Maria thanked the doctor calmly, told him that she would be fine by herself for a moment, and then cried the moment he left the room.

Kevin was in soon after. The tears were still fresh on her cheeks and he didn't even need to ask what she was crying about. He crawled onto the bed next to as best he could and let her cry herself to sleep on his shoulder.

When she woke up again, he was sitting in a chair by her bed, a tablet in his lap and earbuds in his ears. She tried to crane her neck to see what he was watching without disturbing him. All she managed to see was a brief view of the water before he saw she was awake and tried to hide the tablet.

"What was that?" she asked.

"It's probably not anything you need to see just yet."

"What, are you afraid whatever it is will break me or something?"

"I don't know. Will it?"

Maria looked back down at her mangled body. She still hadn't had the time to process any of this, so she couldn't rightfully say how this would affect her in the future. It was entirely possible that the loss of a limb could send her into a terrible depression, that she would be afraid of the sea from now on, that her life would change in drastic and horrible ways that she couldn't predict yet.

But maybe it wouldn't. She believed she was strong enough to take whatever came next.

"No," she said. "Show me."

Kevin raised an eyebrow but said nothing else as he unplugged the earbuds and handed her the tablet. He'd paused it in the middle of a video on YouTube. Maria set it back to the beginning and watched.

It was a clip from one of the major news channels. A quick look at the suggestions on the side of the page showed Maria many more, with sources ranging from the other major news outlets to Inside Edition and even TMZ and Entertainment Tonight. And in half of them her face was prominently displayed in the teaser image.

The one Kevin had been watching was presumably a more measured account of what had happened than would be on some of the other sources. In this particular clip, Wolf Blitzer was interviewing Vandergraf, of all people, who talked animatedly about the events at El Bajo as various shots Gary had taken played over him. Of course, pretty much all of Vandergraf's attempts at scientific explanation were completely wrong but that didn't seem to matter much. His voice was nothing more than additional flavoring for the main course of the video.

And what a dramatic video it turned out to be. There were some of the things that had been filmed earlier, including several shots of the *Tetsuo Maru* sinking. But the big one, the one that they kept replaying over and over, were those final moments of Maria and the Gutsdorfs in the Zodiac. Despite the distance, Gary had managed quite the zoom, and the three of them could clearly be seen in the raft as it raced back to the *Cameron*. Even knowing what was coming, Maria was still shocked when Teddy Bear came up underneath them (although Maria was happy that Wolf Blitzer also seemed hesitant to refer to the hammerhead by that name). The network slowed the footage down, eerily matching the speed at which Maria herself remembered the event. Yet that was where the similarities ended, because in the footage Maria looked far more heroic than she remembered. The raft rose up and there was the monster in all its majestic glory, somehow managing to look even bigger on the screen than she remembered. The Zodiac flew in the air and both of the Gutsdorfs went sprawling, neither of them anywhere close to Teddy Bear. Maria, however, appeared to do some complicated acrobatics in the air and come down on the shark's head. Even though the angle wasn't quite right to show exactly what Maria did to Teddy Bear, there was a visible impact as the shark balked in what might have been pain. The hammerhead dropped back into the ocean and disappeared with Maria following. She couldn't help but notice that the network had chosen to blur out most of the gore on her leg, although she suspected some of the less reputable news sources wouldn't be as scrupulous.

"How many places are showing this stuff?" Maria asked.

"Uh, all of them, as far as I can tell," Kevin said. "The instant we were within wireless range, Vandergraf had uploaded as much of the footage as he possibly could, and it was viral within an hour. I hear he's already gotten five more offers from various networks offering to produce reality shows."

"Ugh, please tell me you're not going to take any of the offers."

"What? Oh no, you misunderstand me. Those five don't involve me. However, three of them would apparently revolve around you."

"Wait, what?"

"Click on one of the other videos," Kevin said. "Probably any of them will do. You'll understand."

She clicked on one from Fox News. An old white guy started complaining about how Maria Quintero was just a liberal ploy to further the climate change conspiracy. Maria had no idea what that had to do with anything, so she clicked on one from MSNBC. An equally old white guy was discussing in a boring monotone how the video of her fighting Teddy Bear was part of the conservative agenda to undermine the environmental movement. Inside Edition was interviewing one of her exes, who lied through his teeth about how adventurous and domineering she was in bed. Entertainment Tonight speculated on what clothing she might be wearing right now in the hospital. The Onion had an article about how she was an action movie cliché.

"Oh my God. What the hell?" she asked.

"You're a celebrity, dear. There have been reporters camped out around the hospital for more than a day, each of them trying to find a way to sneak in here and be the first to interview the amazing marine biologist action hero Maria Quintero."

"You have got to be kidding me. You're the famous scientist, not me. I don't even have my degree yet."

"Maria, you should know by now that people these days treat a degree like it makes you less qualified, not more. You're the one that was caught on tape delivering the final blow to a real life sea monster. I give them facts and figures. You gave them a spectacle. If anything, in this moment at least, people are treating me less like a celebrity scientist and more like your sidekick."

"Oh man. I am not in a good enough mindset yet to deal with this."

"You don't have to. Although now that you're awake you should probably at least release a press statement."

"Jesus Christ fried on a stick." She paused to let herself calm down. She would deal with all that later. For now she still had some questions she wanted answered. "I don't remember anything after hitting the water, and the videos don't show much after that. What happened?"

"You mean other than the fact that we almost lost you?" He said it in a way that very clearly implied that was the only detail that mattered to him. He grabbed her hand, squeezed it, kissed it, and then moved on. "It was a hairy hour or so before the Navy arrived. There wasn't too much damage to your Zodiac, so the Gutsdorfs were able to fish you out of the water before you drowned and got you back to the Cameron. Boleau made a tourniquet and we kept you stable, but you scared us. You scared me."

"Okay, but what about everything else? Given what most of the video clips are concentrating on, you'd think that final shot was the only thing that happened."

"Well of course. You are looking at the American media, after all, and the majority of the people who died weren't American so they don't care. The Mexican news channels are of course concentrating on the bravery of the Mexican Navy in coming to our rescue, even though it was completely over by that point. I scoured the internet looking for anything that the Japanese media is saying. They're the only ones who seem to recognize this whole thing as a tragedy, considering it was one of their ships that sank. Kyo's been very openly speaking out against illegal shark fishing, though. It's too early tell if this incident is going to change anyone's minds."

"Are they blaming us for any of it?"

"Not us specifically, and not even One Planet. Except for a few conspiracy theory websites that think it was all an elaborate false flag attack to do… hell, I don't know. Who can tell what's going on in some of those people's pretzel-twisted minds? But there are some tense international talks going on between Japan and other countries regarding who is to blame and what's going to be done about it. The media does have its one face to plaster all over the place and blame, though, so they don't seem interested in investigating further."

"Mercer?"

Kevin nodded.

"Where is she now?"

"She's in custody, although there's still an argument going on about who gets to take her. She's an American citizen that was with an American crew who committed a terrorist act against Japan in Mexican jurisdiction. It's going to be a while before that get's wrapped up."

"But is she talking?"

"Basically repeating everything she told us. I'm hardly in the loop when it comes to her interrogations, but judging from what little has leaked out I don't think anyone is taking her claims that someone duped her seriously. They think it was just a rogue act by two idiot kids."

"So we still know nothing about who was behind this?"

"No. Nothing."

"What about Smith and his boat? There were plenty of witnesses. Gary must have even gotten some footage."

"A little, but nothing that says anything we need to know.

There's no sign of its wreckage around El Bajo, so it must have gotten away from Teddy Bear, right along with any evidence it might have provided."

"So it's going to stay a mystery," Maria said. "I hate mysteries."

Kevin smiled. "You're a scientist. You love mysteries."

She sighed and nodded. "I love mysteries. I can't wait to get the hell out of here and solve this one. But that leaves only one thread left you haven't talked about. El Bajo."

Kevin's smile got even wider. "I know I shouldn't be smiling given all the horrible things that have happened but, well, they're back. And they seem to be back to normal."

"You mean the hammerheads?"

"The numbers seem to have dwindled a bit over the past few days. I've got Boleau and the Gutsdorfs out monitoring them right now, although Cindy and Simon apparently have somewhere else they need to go sometime soon. They send their love, by the way. But it doesn't look like the numbers are going to drop too much more. Teddy Bear must have attracted hammerheads from all over the world, and El Bajo seems to be their home again. Or at least for as long as mating season goes on. I'm unsure how that's going to work, since Teddy Bear seemed to throw off their normal mating schedule as it was."

"But you really think they're here to stay?"

"It looks that way. We'll have to do a lot more studies, but El Bajo for now looks like the rich ocean habitat it was always supposed to be."

"But what about Teddy Bear? Is she still there? If she is, she could still send the sharks back into a frenzy."

Kevin shook his head. "She's gone, but thanks to the transmitters we know exactly what path she's taking. There's been a lot of discussion by the various governments involved about whether or not she needs to be hunted down and destroyed. We're the only ones with the exact frequencies to the transmitters at the moment though, so we're the only ones who know where she is and how to control her."

"So it worked? The transmitters really do disrupt whatever she was using to control the other sharks?"

"Sometimes yes, sometimes no. It looks like we were definitely on the right track with our theory, but there are odd little inconsistencies that I haven't been able to explain yet. There's still a lot more work that needs to be done, but given that it wasn't my theories or transmitters that did the work, I figured it was only right to offer control over the project back to my buddy. He gracefully accepted, after a whole lot of ungraceful cheering and fist-pumping. I hope you don't mind."

Maria emphatically shook her head and immediately regretted it. Her sense of equilibrium was still off and it made her dizzy. "No, go right ahead. It's not like I bear Teddy Bear any ill will, but my God do I hope I never see her again."

"So far we're only controlling her enough to steer her away from populated areas. Other than that we're letting her be free. We're hoping she'll lead us to more like her, if they're out there."

"Hopefully not too many," Maria muttered. She looked down at the bed sheets and the flat spot where her leg should have been. It was finally starting to dawn on her that she had lost that part of herself forever. And she wasn't entirely sure if it had been worth it. She could have waited and let the Navy take care of Teddy Bear. They would have killed her, but was the life of that creature really worth what she had given up?

Kevin again joined her on the bed and hugged her. Whatever the answer to that question might be, at least she wasn't going to have to answer it alone.

EPILOGUE

Doug Vandergraf had spent the last three days on a whirlwind press tour. He'd been on practically every news magazine show that mattered, agreed with every political talking head that would have him on their show regardless of what side of the political spectrum they were on, and had meetings with no fewer than a dozen networks wanting him to produce their next hot reality show about bored drug-addled housewives or championship comic book collecting. This, thankfully, was his last stop. He'd tried to just get his benefactor to discuss their arrangements over Skype, but Vandergraf had already learned that this person was old school. Only a face-to-face meeting would do, and it had to be in a remote location. But did it really have to be the half-way-around-the-world sort of remote? That struck Vandergraf as going a little overboard.

After many hours flying into South America, Vandergraf was met at the airport by a taciturn man in a limo driver's suit. Although Vandergraf repeatedly asked him where they were going, the driver wouldn't speak, and eventually Vandergraf gave up. They spent many more hours driving, which would have bored Vandergraf to tears if the limo hadn't been equipped with all the champagne he could drink. He was more than a little tipsy when the limo finally stopped somewhere along the coast. Vandergraf thought this might be the rendezvous point, but the limo driver instead showed him to a small private yacht, where again he was expected to wait hours as the yacht made its way to its destination. There was no champagne this time but there was a well stocked bar, to which Vandergraf graciously helped himself.

He'd fallen into an alcohol-induced doze when the yacht jolted to a stop and woke him up. The captain came down just long enough to gruffly inform him they had arrived, then left before Vandergraf could slur a question about where they had arrived at. His contact had not said anything about any of this, but given how much this benefactor had paid Vandergraf for his part in the El Bajo incident, right along with his leap to fame afterward, Vandergraf figured he owed this person at least this much.

When Vandergraf came out on deck, he found that it had become full-on night. There was barely even a moon in the sky to light his way, and the lights on the yacht didn't catch all the shadows on the deck. He thought he could hear sounds in the water like another small boat was tethered to the yacht, but he was wobbly enough on his legs that he didn't want to approach the side and be sure. The captain was nowhere to be seen, but after a few seconds of searching Vandergraf realized he wasn't alone. A woman stood near the back of the yacht, her smart business suit and ridiculously tall high-heels an improbable sight here on the ocean. Yet she had no trouble keeping her balance. Unlike Vandergraf, she seemed at home on the boat's shifting deck.

Vandergraf approached her, but she was standing just outside the lights and he couldn't get a very good look at her face. He recognized the voice when she spoke, though. "Vandergraf, thanks for meeting me here."

"You, huh? Wasn't expecting that. Why are we here, anyway? Couldn't we have this meeting somewhere a little more comfortable? And less prone to make me sea-sick?"

"We could have, but then I wouldn't have been able to give you a sneak peek at what's coming next?"

"Coming next? What do you mean?"

"I mean Teddy Bear was only the first."

"First what? First giant hammerhead shark?"

"The first of my creations, dumbass. You don't think an enormous hammerhead shark that can control other sharks just spontaneously came into existence, do you? I've been busy. Teddy Bear was only a test run, the least interesting of my experiments."

Vandergraf stood dumbfounded. The boat rocked beneath him as though a huge wave had hit it and he stumbled closer to the edge. His benefactor, however, kept her balance perfectly.

"Wait, where even are we?" Vandergraf asked.

"Just off the Galapagos Islands," she said. "It amused me to put one of my laboratories in a place so closely associated with evolution."

The yacht rocked again. It wasn't as though something had hit it. More like something gigantic had just swum underneath it.

"Wait, why are we here?" Vandergraf asked. "If you want me to film whatever you've got hidden here, why wouldn't you have told me in advance? Weren't you happy with how the footage turned out at El Bajo?"

"Oh, I was very happy. You have no idea. Everyone played their part beautifully, even the ones who didn't know what they were a part of. Especially the ones who didn't know." She paused and put a hand to her chin in thought. "Although what happened to Quintero was unexpected. If I want to continue using her, I'll have to give her some incentives. Incentives she's unaware she's receiving, of course."

"So that still doesn't explain why we're here."

The woman stepped out of the shadows and placed a hand on his shoulder. Her tanned face lacked all the youthful innocence of a naïve One Planet volunteer that he had seen on her a few days earlier. Instead the cold, calm look she gave him put years onto her appearance while simultaneously making it hard for him to tell just how old she might really be.

"You are here because you've become a liability," the woman who had been calling herself Cindy Gutsdorf said. "And because I wanted to give my next creature one final test before I declare it ready for the next phase."

And with that she shoved him overboard.

Vandergraf went under and, in the darkness, struggled for several seconds to orient himself and get his head back above the surface. He gasped, trying to expel water from his mouth but only managing to take more in. He knew how to swim well enough to tread water, though, and shortly he found himself floating in a more stable position.

"Whatever you're planning, don't do it!" he screamed as she grasped the railing and looked over the side at him. "You can still use me for whatever you have planned next. You wanted the El

Bajo Incident all over the news. Didn't I deliver?"

"You sure did," the woman said. "A little too well. I do thank you for making Maria Quintero famous. I can use that. But you, on the other hand, were supposed to stay behind the camera. I can't trust someone that hungry to make himself famous. If I let you live, I would never know when you might go out to the world and tell everyone all you know about my brother and me."

"But I don't know anything!"

"Correct. And it's going to stay that way. Oh 'Simon?'" The way she said that last word clearly implied there were supposed to be quotation marks around it. Vandergraf heard something behind him and struggled to face the opposite direction in the water. The man he had known several days earlier as Simon was in a smaller boat right alongside the yacht's captain, who made a point to keep his back to Vandergraf as he listened to an iPod. Simon saw where Vandergraf was looking and smiled. "We promised him that he didn't have to look." He popped one of the captain's earbuds out. "You might want to crank up the volume. There's probably going to be screaming." The captain nodded and put the earbud back in. The music became so loud that Vandergraf could hear it even from here: John Denver's "Calypso."

Simon's grin broadened. "Ha! I couldn't have planned that dramatic irony better if I'd written this movie myself." He reached down into the boat and pulled out what looked like a dead, bloody bird. "Blue-footed booby," he said. "It absolutely *loves* these." And as the air filled with the sultry sounds of John crooning about the joys of sea life, Simon threw the dead bird straight at Vandergraf's face. Vandergraf screeched as the carcass broke his nose and blood ran down his face. He didn't think most of the blood was his, though. He cleaned just enough of the blood off his face to see as Simon pulled out another dead booby and pulled back to pitch it at the yacht.

"Wait, you idiot!" Cindy said. "Wait until I'm back down in the boat with you first. I don't want to be on the yacht when our friend decides it's covered in food."

Simon nodded and said something else, but Vandergraf didn't hear. He was too busy thinking back to what Cindy had just said.

Wait, covered in food?

Something came up from below, the only sign of its approach the churning water surrounding him. Then its mouth closed over his head.

The last thing he heard was Simon singing along with John Denver. He wasn't very good at it.

Maria Quintero and Kevin Hoyt will return in
Galapagos Below

CHECK OUT OTHER GREAT DEEP SEA THRILLERS

MEGA
by Jake Bible

There is something in the deep. Something large. Something hungry. Something prehistoric.
And Team Grendel must find it, fight it, and kill it.
Kinsey Thorne, the first female US Navy SEAL candidate has hit rock bottom. Having washed out of the Navy, she turned to every drink and drug she could get her hands on. Until her father and cousins, all ex-Navy SEALS themselves, offer her a way back into the life: as part of a private, elite combat Team being put together to find and hunt down an impossible monster in the Indian Ocean. Kinsey has a second chance, but can she live through it?

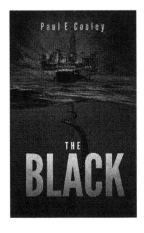

THE BLACK
by Paul E Cooley

Under 30,000 feet of water, the exploration rig Leaguer has discovered an oil field larger than Saudi Arabia, with oil so sweet and pure, nations would go to war for the rights to it. But as the team starts drilling exploration well after exploration well in their race to claim the sweet crude, a deep rumbling beneath the ocean floor shakes them all to their core. Something has been living in the oil and it's about to give birth to the greatest threat humanity has ever seen.

"The Black" is a techno/horror-thriller that puts the horror and action of movies such as Leviathan and The Thing right into readers' hands. Ocean exploration will never be the same."